The Knight Witch: and Other Epic Poems

By S Jayne Bradley

ROOKERY

1st edition 2025

978-1-0671047-0-2 (New Zealand Paperback)
978-1-0671047-1-9 (Ebook)
978-1-0671047-2-6 (Print-on-Demand via Draft2Digital)
978-1-0671047-3-3 (Kindle)
978-1-0671047-4-0 (Amazon Print-on-Demand)

Ride or Die originally printed in North Shore Writers Group Anthology - 2024: Don't Forget to Shut the Gate 979-8300208097. Reprinted here with all permissions.

Acknowledgements

Here we are, a second book, something I never thought I'd ever be saying. It's been an absolute joy writing these new adventures in Rhyme.

To my family, my parents. Dad, I wrote you a western! Mum, now we have a few more horrors to share. To my siblings, Matt and Rachel, thank you for your support.

To Katrina, and Melanie, thank you over 30 years of knowing you and our friendship has only gotten stronger. Here's to another 30 years.

To the NW, always and forever. Endless thanks to the Northshore Writers Group for the feedback, and friendship, that has helped me grow as a writer. Special shout out to Nikky, my Armageddon buddy and the other Armageddon Authors.

Thank you Gillian the editor who really understands my work.

My DnD friends for always being an inspiration, Jennifer, Kass, Bonnie, Sage/Isaac, Ash, Mitch, Anna, Brodie, and Mik.

And finally, to the Orewa Poets, specifically to Robert who helped me get the deal for this second book by having a copy of my first book at readers event my Publisher attended, and also to Sue C, for providing me opportunities to share my knowledge and skills.

So much work went into this, and everyone above has been an integral part of building this new book. Hopefully people enjoy reading it as much as I enjoyed writing it.

Table of Contents

The Knight Witch

Chapter 1

Times have changed; are changing still
We all endure life's tests of will
But horrors come on winter's breath
And with them comes the stench of death

Between the trees and ocean vast
The township stood called Harrow's Mast
A past of blood, Saint Elmo's fire
Foul murder on the Witches' pyre

This town lay somewhere on the coast
A tiny place and far from most
Folks were born and all would stay
In this small town beside the bay

The nights were bright and lit with flames
And wind would call the old Gods' names
Where houses built upon the sand
Had sunk their teeth into the land

The ancient past with tangled roots
In tainted soil grows new shoots
And out of fire, and undue blame
Grew a tree from doubt and shame

A branch of folk that ran so deep
Their names once spoke before you sleep
In tales of dark and wicked spells
And buried things within the wells

Don't go out when full moons wane
Or when the air is cold with rain
If you don't sleep, the witches know
And fly away with you in tow

In Harrow's Mast we lay our scene
Beside the forests dark and green
For when Fern had the sword to fight
This maiden witch became a Knight

Chapter 2

In this town Fern's bones would lay
Like those who'd come before her day
A mother's land, and father's sails
Her ancestors had walked these trails

She had her tools and earned her name
Though village folk would point the blame
When times were hard, her skin was thick
She gave them herbs to do the trick

For on her door, they'd knock so late
And never once did shut the gate
She'd make them drinks and serve them pie
Gave them potions to apply

She'd cure their colds, help mothers nurse
Take their coin and fill her purse
She gained their trust when times were good
And she had thrived there in the wood

Then he came to Harrow's Mast
The preacher, like a winter's blast
He spoke of God and seven hells,
Chided mercy, mocked casting spells

The preacher man with eyes of ice
Had called upon her more than twice
With waifs in tow to hide his sin
He'd buy her potions with a grin

He'd lick his lips and look her way
But she would never let him stay
For he drew evil where he stood
From pulpit through the neighbourhood

He was the weed that grows and chokes
And poisoned words of local folks
By twisting things this witch would do
Beyond the tinctures for the flu

Chapter 3

As months went by, his words took hold
And wicked tales of witches told
Those people who once graced her door
Afraid to visit like before

In the wilds she walked alone
This maiden worked to be the crone
She cast her spells in wood and flame
No portents ever spoke her name

Her days were just what she had planned
No late-night quests, some tasks now banned
But in the hours before her sleep
Into her shadowed books she'd creep

A trace of ancient magic lingers
On pages writ by older fingers
And low would every candle burn
As tone and meaning she would learn

The river ran beside her road
She sang the songs of frog and toad
At water's edge she paused to wait
Her heart it beat a faster rate

On days where skies are dull and grey
Within the reeds this witch would lay
Her fingers dipped into the stream
Fern whispers of her only dream

Then eyes so dark would meet her own
And Fern would cease to be alone
This lady from the water deep
Each other's hearts they hoped to keep

And when the sun began to set
When she has grabbed what she can get
She makes her promise to return
Leaves sandalwood and sage to burn

Her face is bright and ever clear
She walks the streets without much fear
These simpler times will pass her by
And all this witch could do is sigh

Chapter 4

Upon stone floors the preacher stalked
His eyes were sharp, his tongue was forked
He called for God to bless the land
And built foundations on the sand

His robes were black like ocean nights
He talked of good and angels lights
The townsfolk saw his heart as pure
Of his new God they now were sure

No visits to the stones and hill
The voices of Old Gods were still
The angels had now found their way
And with this preacher they would stay

Without the town, she had no gold
And winter nights were getting cold
To Harrow's mast she'd have to go
And what they'd do, she did not know

The seeds of doubt had now been sown
No trust from people she had known
Their visits to her had now ceased
By way of that ignoble Priest

At this time her head held high
There was no truth she must deny
The town still whispered of her kind
And spoke of things left far behind

In Harrow's Mast he wore the crown
The Preacher watched her enter town
He dogged her steps, her movements traced
His interest it had been misplaced

Behind her eyes lay secrets lost
Buried deep beneath the frost
He planned to melt the ice above
And cast a spell to earn her love

Chapter 5

She walked the streets that she knew well
Expected folk to jeer and yell
She fixed her gaze with lifted chin
But still felt goosebumps on her skin

From windows and from doors they'd peek
And no-one made a move to speak
Their eyes were cold, and filled with fear
But as she moved, they'd not draw near

There was a market in this town
With farmers it had some renown
Many things to buy and sell
Some meat and veg, perhaps a spell

Her stall set up to sell her wares
Was only met with scathing stares
But some approached with darting eyes
One man bought herbs in full disguise

By the days end not much had sold
She counted every piece of gold
There was enough to spend the night
Perhaps sell more in morning light

She packed her stall and closed her till
Marked her sales with ink and quill
Towards the inn she made her way
From outside she heard music play

The light spilled out the open door
And people danced upon the floor
As Fern stepped in there was a chill
She would be dead, if looks could kill

But this witch would not be cast out
For no-one had the guts to shout
She'd not be chased away by shame
The Barman took her coin the same

Chapter 6

She went upstairs to rest her head
Then locked the door and checked her bed
No poison, traps or things that burn
But still she felt her stomach churn

The bread was hard, but not the worst
And sleep it wouldn't come at first
When all was dark and lights grew dim
The chance of restful sleep was slim

Outside the inn loud footsteps fell
A voice called out, "She'll burn in hell!"
And down below the barman called
"Fuck off!" and the preacher stalled

"Here you cannot build your pyre,
And to your bed you must retire,"
A cry rang out a stern request
The preacher man he was obsessed

"Relinquish her I'll surely not"
"Transgressions mean that she must rot,"
What passed between were idle threats
Neither man would have regrets

The footsteps faded down the street
The preacher's task still incomplete
And Fern she knew he would make good
To have her over burning wood

When morning came, she knew to go
She'd thank the barman, let him know
That kindness was its own reward
 And thanked him for his strength and sword

She sold some things as she left town
And kept her head and eyes cast down
Her movement slow, her baggage light
And she would make it home by night

Chapter 7

She held her books close to her heart
Their pages were a work of art
She kept them locked from prying eyes
To lend them out would not be wise

So deep inside her little house
She slept tucked in just like a mouse
Her dreams would take her far away
To places she could never stay

The stars came out in blackened skies
And waited for the sun to rise
Beside her door he lay in wait
Taking time and testing fate

He stepped inside and closed the door
She wouldn't be alone much more
His hands were light, his fingers deft
All he had to do was theft

He found the books, his heart's desire
Placed behind the hearth and fire
One burnt hand had been his price
And that was fixed with lumps of ice

The ancient pages would be turned
By hands that had been badly burned
He knew not what spell he could cast
He knew he had to take them fast

Her frozen heart he soon would claim
Within him burned the hottest flame
He'd take her from her lofty perch
And wed her before God and church

There was a chant, one incantation
That promised power and creation
Scribed in ink of bloody red
Its darkish words had filled his head

Chapter 8

When the rooster's cry was heard
Within her room the woman stirred
The sky was blue, but all felt wrong
The feeling had been growing strong

But up she sat and fetched her food
Though she wasn't in the mood
She stuffed her face and glanced outside
A storm was coming with the tide

She checked the time and started chores
The chickens fed, and mopped the floors
And gathered herbs and fixed the gates
She washed her clothes and then her plates

She scrubbed her hands and then her face
Mending socks and threading lace
But something nagged and something nicked
Her thoughts escaped as clocks had ticked

Then Fern, about to slice some bread
And darn some stockings while she fed
But someone had removed the stone
And took what had been hers alone

Goosebumps ran across her skin
Who had dared to step within
Her anger beat this new despair
From now on she would tread with care

She searched her home to be assured
That someone else had now procured
These ancient tomes of magic lore
That they were not here anymore

Fern saw the prints beneath her own
In the mud and mossy stone
The marks they lead to Harrow's Mast
And she would have to get there fast

Chapter 9

The trees had whispered rustled words
And passed their secrets to the birds
Who called out to the Witch's ear
In the hopes that she would hear

Upon the hill a fire burned
Inside her gut her stomach churned
The smell of burning demon's ire
As wood was thrown onto the fire

With wringing hands, she chased the smoke
And chanted words the old god's spoke
She knew not what this man had cast
But sure as hell it was his last

As trees stepped back around the glade
She understood the mess he'd made
"Oh preacher man with heart of coal,
Cease before it claims your soul."

And as he stood, his cross laid bare
With white streaks in his jet black hair
His eyes of ash and mottled green
His grin was wide and so unclean

"By God's own grace, I earned my prize
I see it deep within your eyes,
Oh maiden of the wilding wood
I think you have misunderstood."

Fern raised her hands to break the spell
And cast this monster back to hell
But as the words escaped her lips
Her hands had fallen to her hips

The preacher stared with vacant eyes
Her mouth made an 'O' of surprise
The priest's intent it was exclaimed
A demon of a spell was named

Chapter 10

The name was old and one she knew
A curse not used in witches' brew
It took a hold of soul and skin
Burning mortal flesh within

The spell was dark and brought the storm
A demon rose in human form
Its eyes of ice and burning flame
To call it you must say its name

The spell itself a warning tale
To those who thought they could prevail
 It also held the curse's cure
To break it, one's soul must be pure

The story told of knights betrayed
Of warlords and of debts unpaid
The knight was sworn on bended knee
And on his death he would be free

A queen once crowned had cast the spell
And with his sword, her king, he fell
She buried deep his rotting bones
There was no dawn for broken thrones

Her knight returned from errand true
An oath he swore, the spell, undo
With silver sword he raised his blade
This demon's debt would soon be paid

With one swing he took her head
Still pure of heart he left her dead
The demon smoke it fell to dust
And it was gone in just one gust

The knight he bowed and on one knee
He'd say a prayer and then he'd flee
There was no throne left to defend
And it was all a rotten end

Chapter 11

The Preacher man, he called her name
Upon her life he'd laid his claim
But she was wise and quicker still
She knew there would be blood to spill

The preacher's feelings were misplaced
So through the woods with greatest haste
Through brush and scrub and fallen stone
This task was one she'd do alone

She had a knife for cutting bread
A dagger to make chickens dead
But had no sword, no shining blade
It was a thing her kind forbade

Her craft was one of earth and rain
It was not meant for dealing pain
But she must grow and find her strength
And knew she'd go to any length

She was no martyr, nor a saint
Nor was she frail, she would not faint
She'd taken lives, though small indeed
This witch was never filled with greed

A story that her grandma told
When she was barely five years old
Within a lake so dark and green
A lady dwelled so deep, unseen

With reeds for hair and dark brown eyes
The water was the best disguise
The witch had seen her in the rushes
And on her she had held her crushes

To the lake where grass meets sand
Where water nestles to the land
The Witch sat down upon the shore
And hoped to see her crush once more

Chapter 12

The witch sat down on sand and stones
And rested on her weary bones
She knew the spell that she must break
And trap the demon now awake

She stepped out in the misty lake
Fallen leaves tossed in her wake
The water was so crystal clear
She walked in deep with little fear

Across her leg a hand had brushed
Around the lake the air had hushed
A bird cried out in distant skies
Then she saw those dark brown eyes

A copper face from waves emerged
A warmth within her heart had surged
The lady stood in robes of green
As elegant as any queen

"Oh Witch of woods, you tread my shore,
As if you'd knock upon a door,"
Her lips had curved into a smile
"I hope you're here to stay awhile,"

The Witch stood tall, and self-assured
Into the lake she'd not be lured
"A spell was cast, I need a blade
This demon loosed, it must be slayed,"

The lady smiled, and bowed her head
The witch felt cold, just like the dead
"I have the sword that you have sought,
There is a cost for evil wrought."

She sank below the lake once more
The witch now shivered to her core
The sun was sinking to the trees
And Fern herself about to freeze

Chapter 13

The lady she had then returned
Her dark eyes blazed as if they burned
"A knight is made when need is dire,
Testing steel and trial by fire"

And in her grasp, she held the blade
From starlight it was deftly made
Its edge was sharp, and finely hewn
To have this sword it was a boon

The witch reached out, but then recoiled
Perhaps this moment had been spoiled
The lady smirked, "I have my price,
I do not gain if I play nice,"

The Witch stood firm and then knelt down,
She wasn't deep enough to drown
"What would you ask of me this night?
I will make sure it is done right."

The lady sank and met her gaze
Her face was cold, her eyes ablaze
"There is one gift you can bestow."
The witch she felt her heart aglow

"A kiss between a knight and maid,
And then consider your debt paid."
The witch's cheeks had then burned red
Flustered by what the maid had said

Fern closed her eyes and then leaned in
Her heart was making her head spin
A gentle hand upon her cheek
Her mouth agape as if to speak

A touch of cold upon her lips,
And sturdy hands upon her hips
Familiar need, a longing ache
The kiss was deeper than the lake

Chapter 14

The knight then stood with blade in hand
And set her feet upon the land
Then as the Lady waved goodbye
Fern heaved a lonely lovestruck sigh

Her footfalls hit the sand and mud
Tonight, for her there would be blood
Though she was wet and feeling cold
She would not let this chill take hold

Upon the hill, the fire burned
And deep inside her stomach churned
She saw the townsfolk in the glade
And to the Old Gods then she prayed

The Knight Witch cursed in ancient tongues
The air was hot inside her lungs
Sparks shot out from on the pyre
The smoke and flames were getting higher

She held the sword to catch the light
For she was spoiling for a fight
She had to win to break the spell
Or face the very depths of hell

The townsfolk saw her eyes so bright
The glinting sword cut through the night
Below she saw the ocean vast
And hoped to put this in the past

She saw the preacher man deformed
He stood before the crowd and stormed
His teeth were points and eyes were ice
If there was debt, he'd paid it thrice

His hands were twisted into claws
Their sharpness gave the Knight Witch pause
This demon would no longer preach
And godliness was out of reach

Chapter 15

Around her cold the storm wind swirled
Through her auburn hair it curled
Her jaw was set, her eyes were steel
Before her she would make him kneel

And from the crowd she soon emerged
About to have this demon purged
She raised her sword and called its name
"Upon this town you have no claim."

Its rumpled skin was tinted red
And smelled just like the newly dead
It hissed and spat without a word
She had no doubt that it had heard

It turned to her with eyes of hate
And in them she witnessed her fate
The wind blew hard, the earth it shook
It was just like a story book

It loomed so tall and out of place
Rage was etched upon its face
It leered at Fern and licked its jaws
Then reached out with its jagged claws

As it drew near, she swung the blade
Blood was drawn, the demon brayed
Its face had stretched into a grin
And fire flared beneath its skin

In one swift leap the Knight Witch lunged
Into its flesh her weapon plunged
It bared its teeth as it drew back
 And then it poised for its attack

Around Fern, all the townsfolk saw
And of their witch they were in awe
Her healing hands now primed to fight
And with her silvered blade she'd smite

Chapter 16

The demon grew in shape and size
And fire burned within its eyes
It leaped again with snapping jaws
And orange sparks burst from its claws

Its face drew near, she smelled the smoke
Unless she held her breath she'd choke
She drew herself to fighting stance
And moved like she was at a dance

The blade gleamed bright, like fire shone
But with a swipe she landed prone
Above her loud the demon growled
It raised its head, in triumph howled

Its open maw had dripped with drool
At once she thought herself a fool
And from the crowd a rock was thrown
The demon then let out a groan

And as it struck the message clear
The townsfolk would not bend in fear
A shout rang out and more rocks flew
As it recoiled, was then she knew

She scrambled up, regained her stance
Fern wouldn't let it win by chance
"Oh foulest beast, no god, nor man,
Come and fight me if you can,"

It hunched its back just like a cat
Prepared itself for more combat
Above them thunder cracked and roared
Then it didn't rain; it poured

The fire dimmed but did not shrink
And water cleared some of the stink
The witch then raised her sword once more
And she looked like a knight of yore

Chapter 17

Below the hill, the Church bells rang
And with her mighty blade she sprang
The blade cut once and then once more
It sparkled in the rain of gore

But every strike was true indeed
And magically it sensed her need
And blow by blow the beast shrank back
Until its fiery eyes turned black

It howled and bayed then fell still
The Knight Witch went in for the kill
With both her hands, the blade she raised
The final blow it would be praised

As burning coals replaced the flame
She uttered once the demon's name
And cursed it as the fires died
There was no place for it to hide

Its body crumpled on the ground
No more the beast would make a sound
It fell to ash and what remained
Was not a thing that could be named

The preacher man with eyes of blue
His days of scripture were now through
As church bells ceased their sullen tones
The townsfolk went to rest their bones

The Knight Witch followed head held high
Today was not her day to die
She did not need much of a search
And found her books within the church

She held them close and home she went
The battle left her worn and spent
With every step she stopped to yawn
When she arrived, it was near dawn

Chapter 18

Her house was cold when she got home
It smelled of herbs and fresh dug loam
She tucked her books back on their shelf
Then she went to bed herself

The sword she placed beside the door
She wouldn't need it anymore
Once she had slept, when fast would break
She would return it to the lake

Deep in the hours of the night
She awoke when stars were bright
The lady stood all dressed in gold
Despite the chill she wasn't cold

To see the Witch, the Lady smiled
The Knight Witch indeed looked wild
Untidy hair and wounds to heal
And not yet on an even keel

The Knight Witch bowed and grabbed the sword
It was no prize, and no reward
And to her knees the knight then dropped
Despite her words, she'd not be stopped

"I return to you the gift bestowed
Nothing lost and nothing owed,"
The Knight Witch gazed into her eyes
That seemed so young and yet so wise

The lady took the blade in hand
"My Bravest Fern, you have to stand,"
The Knight Witch stood and bowed her head
The lady lifted it instead

Her hands were soft and cold as frost
With eyes so dark one would get lost
"There is one thing my Knight Witch missed."
The lady and her maiden kissed

A Woman's Work is Never Done

Her hair is tied in curls and clips
And rouge is spread upon her lips
Her eyes are bright, her smile is wide
And all her fears must be denied

Her house is nice and painted blue
The shutters are a reddish hue
The lawn is cut, the fence is stone
She's pleased to call this house her own

Outside the sky is lit up green
She knows of course what this will mean
She checks the locks, and bars the door
Puts caltrops on the kitchen floor

Her dress is clean and freshly pressed
She has no time to sit and rest
There are her chores and children too
And after that still more to do

Across the skies the clouds would shift
Curfews they would never lift
But that is neither here nor there
When she must choose what she should wear

Her children sleeping in their beds
Tucked in tight, they rest their heads
And dreams will come with fitful sleep
While trying not to scream and weep

She checks the windows locked and barred
'Cause what she'd seen had left her scarred
Her happy smile it shall not fade
Even if her nerves are frayed

Her heels are sharp as are her nails
She takes a breath and then exhales

She pours her man the stiffest drink
And helps him as he tries to think

His shoulders rubbed and back is scratched
And still this man remains detached
He'll ask her thoughts, but she'll abstain
His world was never her domain

He takes the drink and waves her off
With a glance and then a scoff
With proof of feminine restraint
She will oblige without complaint

He sips his gin and then complains
"No whiskey, love," she then explains
Her high heels clacking on the floor
As she retreats out through the door

Her bed is made, but she won't sleep
She has a house that she must keep
The fence is high, the gate is barred
Her life could sometimes be quite hard

Her husband's voice, he calls for her
What he could want, she wasn't sure
When she walks in, he looks her way
He gestures for his wife to stay

She takes a seat and gives her smile
It's one she's not used in a while
He rolls his eyes and sips his gin
She sees his patience wearing thin

He talks to her as if she's dumb
And to his jibes she is now numb
And as he speaks with grace and poise
She is alerted by a noise

He sees that her attention's lost
He turns to ice and breathes his frost

The Knight Witch

"You never care for what I say,"
His drunken mind now led astray

But noises leave her quite distracted
Protocols must be enacted
 Her eyes are wide as she stares out
And her beloved gives a shout

He wants to talk and have her hear
But something else is drawing near
She grabs his tools, prepares to fight
 And soon will set the gin alight

Her hair is curled, her lips are red
Her beating heart cuts through the dread
A disk appears in glowing green
It has a strange metallic sheen

With curtains closed and lights dimmed low
 Outside the dark sky starts to glow
She checks her kids and lets them rest
So if they run, they'll do their best

Her husband calls for one more gin
It is a fight she cannot win
His will of iron cannot be beat
She'll pour his last and then retreat

The broken glass came as a shock
Her husband fired off his Glock
And on his feet he made his stand
Until the creature ate his hand

Tall and thin with gleaming eyes
Her husband he had tried to rise
The creature lunged and ate his face
She hoped to die with much more grace

It bit down hard, her husband screamed
Unable now to be redeemed

He wet his pants, his limbs they flailed
And her relief was thinly veiled

Her husband made a good main course
This end was better than divorce
His body landed with a thud
Jagged teeth now dripping blood

The creature hissed and looked to her
And then she made the chainsaw purr
With a shout, she swung the saw
And sliced right through the creature's jaw

Its blood was blue and flecked with green
And it would be a bitch to clean
She checked her face in shattered glass
If she must die, she'd die with class

Despite the spray of blue and green
Her dress it still remained pristine
And in her heels she chased the sound
Saw where the creatures struck the ground

By the door she lay in wait
She heard the breaking of the gate
A few steps back and she prepared
She braced herself, her teeth were bared

The door soon broke and they charged through
Then blood was spilled in shades of blue
Their skin was split by caltrops spikes
And this was just one of her strikes

The lights went out, as they came in
And then she smashed her husband's gin
She lit a flame and watched it catch
Then she tossed away the match

She let the chainsaw roar to life
Like butter with a hot steel knife

But then she heard her children cry
'Twould rend her soul to see them die

She raced upstairs towards their room
Into darkness, into gloom
The bedroom door was open wide
She prayed they'd found a place to hide

Then she heard another call
Somewhere further down the hall
There came a sound of breaking tile
What had these creatures dared defile?

But when she reached the bathroom door
The creature dead upon the floor
A pool of blood, its head was crushed
Into the room the mother rushed

Inside the tub her young son hid
Her daughter smashed the cistern lid
Upon its head with one hard blow
The bravest kid she'd ever know

In the lull they grabbed their gear
And from the house they fled in fear
Her husband's Jaguar had their stuff
Packed for when things got too rough

The moral is don't suffer fools
Grab the gin and gardening tools
You can be strong to fit your needs
And you can kill it if it bleeds

S Jayne Bradley

Ride or Die

The clouds hung heavy and close to the ground
The thunder rumbled an ominous sound
There had been no rain, at least not just yet
But Joe, soon enough, would be getting wet

He'd ridden his bike for quite a few years
Now it was so old and grinding its gears
Delivering pizza, flowers, and mail
Through wind, sleet and rain, he would never fail

But times they had changed, and luck had run thin
Becoming a game that he couldn't win
His bills had piled up, repairs had been made
And all warning signs, they must be obeyed

Still Joe worked hard, and he carried the most
But soon his old bones would give up the ghost
Business had slowed, thanks to Amazon vans
'Next Day' delivery had screwed up his plans

He took on the jobs he knew not to take
The cash was too good to be a mistake
He could not deny what business was done
He always stayed safe; he knew when to run

And just like the storm, this new job had come
He would not refuse, he wasn't that dumb
The uniformed man who worked the first floor
Did not tell him why it was by his door

With chills on his skin, he then went inside
He found a note tucked where the box was tied
There was a short list, a large wad of cash
With all his bills it was gone in a flash

Address included, with a date and time
It did seem as though there would be no crime

The Knight Witch

But who was the sender, why was it here?
Doubts crept in his mind, manifested his fear

There had been no name, and no addressee
Never told who the receiver would be
And on the fine print his brown eyes had scanned
He took in each word, so he'd understand

He read the rules twice to get it all straight
Deliver it quick and then close the gate
Left cash on the bench, a note for his wife
Then he prepared for the ride of his life

He had a few hours to get the box there
To miss this one chance, he would never dare
He checked out his map, a new route was made
By Gods of thunder, he wasn't afraid

With helmet in place, and his rusted bike
A second to watch the lightning bolt strike
The streets were all empty, no-one around
Hiding from rain and the thunderous sound

He'd never once been to this house before
He'd not rung the bell or knocked on the door
If the local tales were true to be told
The owners had left, the house never sold

When he would arrive, to rules he'd adhere
His stomach twisting and turning with fear
He walked to the gate, the rain it had come
It beat on his head like pounding a drum

His coat kept him warm, but was soaked before long
And Joe's trembling nerves were soon feeling wrong
What could be seen, far beyond the black gate
Was he in danger, was he tempting fate?

The gate was quite tall and locked by a chain
He jiggled the latch, and blinked away rain

It swung open wide, and gave a loud clang
And into the storm the hollow sound rang

He then closed the gate and walked to the stoop
The driveway was long, and it had a loop
So up to the door, Joe knew what to do
Knock only three times and wait for the cue

If no-one appeared, he should ring the bell
Be patient and wait, it may take a spell
Joe stood by the door and knocked, one two three
His heart and his soul then told him to flee

No-one had answered, so Joe pressed the bell
The dread and foreboding, he could not quell
No footsteps, no creaking, no sound at all
Only the rain that did not cease to fall

The door opened wide with a burst of air
And Joe could see that nobody was there
He leaned his head in and peaked far inside
So many places for monsters to hide

Wall lamps were dim with a light that was gold
The wallpaper thin, the curtains were old
Threadbare and worn, the carpet was stained
The house appeared clean, but barely maintained

Joe went inside, and reluctantly so
This wasn't a place he'd usually go
The rules he was given, were not very clear
Of what he must do if no-one was here

Deeper he ventured, into the hall
He lifted his voice and gave out a call
Then something moved, above it had shifted
Joe, he stepped back, and his eyes he lifted

He had listened hard and called out again
For seconds it seemed his shout was in vain

The Knight Witch

When it occurred, that strange sound overhead
He took some steps back before he stopped dead

Rumbles and gurgles like thunder outside
Were getting close with a crunch and a slide
The breath that was held escaped with a gasp
The package he held then fell from his grasp

The cold in his blood had started to spread
From in his boots, to the top of his head
His hair stood on end, he then stumbled back
The thing on the stairs was slimy and black

Reaching out claws, the creature drew near
Joe he was staring and shaking with fear
He moved for the door, it reached for his throat
Its oozing, black flesh did bubble and bloat

Joe saw his face, its surface reflected
He couldn't move as his brain directed
The thunder outside it cracked like a whip
As into this thing he started to slip

Its touch was cold as the rain from the sky
Deep down Joe knew he was going to die
Its hunger he felt as it touched his skin
Burning like ice and defiling like sin

His death in this house it was not to be
So with all his might Joe ripped himself free
He fell to the floor, still covered in slime
It wouldn't have him, at least not this time

He scrambled across the carpeted floor
Dragged his own body toward the front door
It burbled and howled, without its fresh meat
With all of his strength, Joe got to his feet

It slunk close behind and splattered its ooze
Spraying poor Joe and the back of his shoes

He rushed out the door, and down the front stoop
Dropping his coat that was covered with goop

He raced down the path and out of the gate
And scooped up his bike, it wasn't too late
He jumped on his wheels and started to race
His heart and his feet were moving at pace

The whiz of the wheels and clink of the chain
Mixed with the sound of the hard falling rain
He forgot bruises, the pain was a dream
If he opened his mouth, he'd need to scream

At every sharp turn he flicked back his gaze
The sky had turned black, the streets were a maze
A cascade of wet from trees overhead
He caught up his breath and wished for his bed

He got to his door, the storm still mid-rage
The lift coming down it took such an age
But into his home, he finally stepped
Joe grabbed a clean towel from where they were kept

Dinner was waiting and still piping hot
The day's dark events were nearly forgot
But as he lay down to sleep oh so late
He asked himself this, "Did I shut the gate?"

A Robot Heart

When man was made, and God stood by
To watch these creatures live and die
He spoke the word and understood
That man was made for bad and good

But what he saw from far above
That these small things were filled with love
And now he watched with endless ire
As they cast God into the fire

Then from the ash the humans built
Upon the rocks and on the silt
A world of chrome, a world of steel
And things that had no way to feel

A robot with its heart of stone
Was made to work hard, all alone
With his brains of chips and wires
He sought to create new desires

This robot knew of human ways
Knew how and when the music plays
Picked fresh roses, daisies too
And understood an, "I love you"

His metal eyes could calculate
The aspects of a twist of fate
And learn the function of a heart
Where love was an integral part

The simple tasks had filled his day
There was no leave, just bills to pay
He had a shop where he made tools
For those who build the homes and schools

He watched young families change and grow
It was a thing he'd never know

The tools he made were built not born
This thought had left him quite forlorn

This was a dream he'd had before
And one he would cease to ignore
He'd change himself to learn desire
To know the heat of inner fire

He planned to make himself a heart
And it would be a work of art
So, like old Gods, he worked with clay
It only took him half a day

This red glazed heart it would not beat
It wasn't quite a source of heat
And did not change the way he'd think
It did not lift and did not sink

As time had passed and he stayed cold
Inside him this clay heart had rolled
It rattled in his empty chest
Became a source of others' jest

His metal hands had longed to feel
Make the world around him real
Upon the shelf he placed this heart
And had to go back to the start

And while at work he saw her there
With eyes of gold and silver hair
Her form it moved with simple grace
This robot tried to keep her pace

If heart he had, it should feel light
Like mist she moved just out of sight
He chased her still, ran out the door
To him she was who he'd adore

He saw she worked inside a store
A clothing shop, and nothing more

She'd serve and then she'd give a smile
And he would linger for a while

A shoulder touch to turn her head
It felt like he was made of lead
The strength of love was not deterred
His tubes and wires softly purred

Her voice was soft, she met his gaze
And he could stare at her for days
He touched her hand, and held it tight
Then he watched her skin turn white

She pushed him back and looked away
And told him that he could not stay
A guard stepped in and grabbed his arm
Reminded him to do no harm

He did oblige, was not deterred
And for him no real crime occurred
He could return if he so chose
A new idea inside him rose

He understood with clearer eyes
He could not win her like a prize
Love must be earned or built with care
He should not be so laisser-faire

A second heart it must be made
An organ that would match his trade
So out of steel and not of loam
He'd build this heart of shining chrome

On God's own shoulders, he would stand
He'd soon have one who'd hold his hand
He worked for days and many nights
And worked until he had no lights

Into his chest this new heart fit
He'd made a place for it to sit

The lights stayed dull and failed to glow
What had gone wrong he would soon know

Within the store, all by herself
On a stool beside a shelf
The robot man he then approached
And said the lines himself had coached

But things did not go as he planned
She did not take him by the hand
Her voice was harsh and as she screamed
The noise it shattered all he'd dreamed

The guard returned and filled with rage
The robot knew not to engage
He was expulsed from her small store
Told not to come back anymore

He had supposed that he was cold
Perhaps he had been much too bold
No, not a dream but simple fact
There was a piece that he had lacked

His hands and heart were burning cold
And with her flesh they could not fold
Instead of wires he'd try once more
He'd use what he had not before

The woman walked without a care
Again, he chased her through the square
Into the sun and bustling street
His heart of steel and wires beat

And there she was to do her work
Beside her store he knew to lurk
And kinder words he had not spoke
Within him a new thought awoke

He saw the thing that he desired
From in his core he was inspired

The Knight Witch

To him she was the strangest thing
The smallest hope to which he'd cling

A beating heart's a heavy price
And feelings can be imprecise
This robot thought his love professed
And reached a hand into her chest

S Jayne Bradley

Rats of New York

The garbage truck will haul for days
Miasmic stench a welcome friend
In this misty morning haze
There is more trash around the bend
To heaven garbage men ascend
And when they start to decompose
Their funerals most will attend
And that's the way the story goes

There is one thing that you should know
This work is hard and poorly paid
Times are bad when cash won't flow
When contracts cease to be obeyed
That's when folk should be afraid
When garbage stays, it brings them woes
The Union men start their crusade
And that's the way the story goes

This set up always has its place
And as it builds, it's ended fast
The Mayor has to save his face
And maybe there are new laws passed
Though most folks knew it would not last
But from the heap new worries rose
Though small, their numbers were now vast
But that's the way the story goes

As night time comes on scuttling feet
And twitching noses, teeth that bite
From the alleys and from the street
They chew on anything in sight
They will be hungry through the night
People wake to cries of crows
All other birds had taken flight
And that's the way the story goes

The outdoor cats they stood no chance
And owners were filled with regret
While things seemed fine at their first glance
They'd realise they had lost a pet
They hadn't seen the worst just yet
Events cascade like dominoes
It was a time they'd not forget
And that's the way the story goes

While mourning was par for this course
No warning raised for cats now lost
Few gathered to reveal a source
Man felt that no boundary was crossed
And over this the truth was glossed
Officials had turned up their nose
All complaints were mostly tossed
And that's the way the story goes

The next night saw some windows break
All food left out had been devoured
Destruction left in all its wake
For culprits everywhere was scoured
Trust in cops it had now soured
Incompetence it really shows
Despite them being overpowered
And that's the way the story goes

Nothing gained and nothing solved
While down below the folks were scared
The higher ups were all absolved
And everyone was unprepared
People fought and tensions flared
Without much thought the case they'd close
It seemed like no-one really cared
And that's the way the story goes

Then one fine day all hell broke loose
In daylight broad, the rats came out
Like lightning from the hands of Zeus
From midtown they had seemed to spout

Some folk fought for fame and clout
Just to be chewed from head to toes
On buildings blood had stained the grout
And that's the way the story goes

The carnage left for all to see
It had been covered by the press
The cyclic news it had been key
Reduce the impact of this mess
But on the ground there was no guess
There was so much they could expose
But all attempts had no success
And that's the way the story goes

As each day passed it all got worse
The rats they nested in Time Square
There was no way they would disperse
Their smell was filling up the air
Leaders hid the whole affair
Despite the work, their number grows
Soon the rats were everywhere
And that's the way the story goes

Their little feet had grown so bold
And somehow they had broken through
Upon white walls and seats of gold
They crawled in homes owned by the few
The upper crust caused much ado
How much, the news would not disclose
But those on high they found a crew
And that's the way the story goes

The hired hands had planned for days
The rats they seemed to have no end
And buildings they would have to raze
Much of Downtown they couldn't mend
It was so hard to comprehend
The PD now had reached new lows
The law's long arm it would extend
But that's the way the story goes

The plan was made then blow by blow
The poison traps had now been laid
How much they'd used no-one would know
This toxic stuff it had no grade
The pros and cons carefully weighed
Before they went and sprayed the hose
The danger had not been conveyed
But that's the way the story goes

The folk who got it in the face
They did not make the night's news cast
Their agony was out of place
In towers rich folk weren't aghast
When below work was half-assed
Because of laws they'd not impose
In tests the poison hadn't passed
And that's the way the story goes

The New York Mayor took a backseat
And told his town to make it right
This scourge of rats they could be beat
And they were up for quite a fight
But he remained far out of sight
Against the words he did propose
But not at all was he contrite
And that's the way the story goes

The Opposition made their stance
In verbal combat they had met
Plans they promised would advance
Had higher costs that made them sweat
The price was more than their regret
So in the end they'd not oppose
The best laid plans became a threat
And that's the way the story goes

A curfew they would now enforce
No matter what the process cost
The PD they had no remorse
And anyone they would accost

No hearts of theirs they could defrost
As all the cops did as they chose
Around these men could not be bossed
But that's the way the story goes

It was a hero that would wake
And never had he been a coward
This feeling he just couldn't shake
And at his teachers he had glowered
When praise and gifts on him had showered
His skill with flutes they said it glows
Left him feeling quite empowered
And that's the way the story goes

Around his tunes the rats revolved
Many lives had now been spared
Their bad behaviour had evolved
But in one 'burb, no-one was scared
No bites, no scratch, not one had dared
Less and less remained as foes
The music played, the rats just stared
And that's the way the story goes

It seemed as if there was a truce
But soon enough the word got out
The hows and whos they would deduce
The rich began to cry and pout
That all their homes had been left out
And promised it would come to blows
They called him such a lay-about
But that's the way the story goes

They gave their case and made their plea
They promised cash to an excess
The Mayor came in on bended knee
The boy felt things he'd not express
Upon this gift they would impress
That payment would decrease his woes
But if they could, they'd pay him less
And that's the way the story goes

Before this task he would rehearse
The lilting notes hung in the air
And all the while they would converse
Making plans that were not fair
For their intent was not to share
He'd not complain they would suppose
It was a cross he'd have to bear
And that's the way the story goes

The boy then did as he was told
Behind him rats had formed a queue
He worked until the night was cold
With coughs and sniffs, he caught a flu
But tomorrow he would start anew
He drank some tea with hips of rose
Exhausted he would push on through
And that's the way the story goes

This could have gone so many ways
On kindness most folk would depend
And some survive on heaped on praise
A currency you cannot spend
But you should do as you intend
For what you sow is now what grows
Comeuppance gets you in the end
And that's the way the story goes

He marched the streets with rats in tow
The music spread without much aid
And nothing seemed to break the flow
Through the muck he had to wade
With tired hands the boy still played
While coughing with his runny nose
But from his path he never strayed
And that's the way the story goes

Then step by step became his pace
And under skies now overcast
The higher ups gave him no grace
Because results were needed fast

But old New York was far too vast
And working hard without repose
His body simply would not last
And that's the way the story goes

From Red Hook to East Thirteenth Street
He did not miss a single site
Each resident he'd wave and greet
He even met one socialite
And everything was looking bright
This chapter was about to close
But joy would prove to be finite
And that's the way the story goes

It had become strange circumstance
Perhaps some needs had not been met
This boy had simply missed his chance
Despite stone contracts being set
The mayor had then hedged his bet
And made his promises to those
Rich folks who wouldn't pay their debt
But that's the way the story goes

The boy talked 'til his voice was hoarse
In public streets he would accost
His clothes still rough, his words were coarse
All complaints again were tossed
The work was done for no high cost
Each claim the Mayor would oppose
The boy knew he was double crossed
And that's the way the story goes

They promised that they wouldn't flake
Refusals left him feeling soured
The boy had hoped for a mistake
But over him their lawyers towered
Behind their legs the rich folk glowered
This was the way of CEOs
You give an inch, they feel empowered
And that's the way the story goes

The situation soon devolved
And nothing could have been repaired
all talks were left unresolved
 Nothing in the news was aired
The public showed that they had cared
Donations and some gifts with bows
Their gratitude had been declared
And that's the way the story goes

The CEOs had no excuse
The process slow was still drawn out
And rich folks' answers were obtuse
Each time he tried to call them out
But it was nothing but a rout
As in his face these doors would close
He had a plan to carry out
And that's the way the story goes

One more chance to pay their fee
A warning from those they oppress
The words he spoke contained no glee
From on the street to local press
These elements would coalesce
A gentle threat he would compose
But still the boy had no success
And that's the way the story goes

The course of justice now perverse
And all New York was now aware
A path that they cannot reverse
His voice so calm he would declare
That those who owed should now prepare
Against a wall these threats he throws
And it is more than he can bear
But that's the way the story goes

For the rich the bell had tolled
And those whose claimed their blood was blue
For all the cards this boy did hold
Proved that carnage would soon ensue

Because their debts they would eschew
This was a road the rich folk chose
It was a day that they would rue
And that's the way the story goes

The boy he played and all would gaze
And many folks they would attend
This young boy's march would cause delays
The status quo he would upend
The cops they could not comprehend
A protest they could not enclose
He knew what message this would send
And that's the way the story goes

Around them time had seemed to slow
Because this debt had not been paid
The price was more than what they'd owe
With teeth much sharper than a blade
Then into mansions they'd invade
Far beneath the circling crows
So all the while the music played
And that's the way the story goes

On what they fed there was no trace
And many stood and stared aghast
For what would come they'd have to brace
A hunger that was unsurpassed
Their claws and jaws were much too fast
With blood that dripped from tail to nose
Upon the news this was broadcast
And that's the way the story goes

On high-born flesh the rats would eat
Devouring each and every bite
A taste for bone and tender meat
Consuming everything in sight
None of them slept well that night
For fear of death it overthrows
The thought that they were in the right
But that's the way the story goes

Down the street the boy would dance
His flute, their squeaks, a fine duet
The rats in tow, he would advance
The boy he barely broke a sweat
His music no-one would forget
And as the rhythm never slows
Still no dollar seen as yet
And that's the way the story goes

He played until his voice was hoarse
And struggled through the morning frost
There was no law here to enforce
The PD's plans had all been tossed
New Yorkers knew the cops had lost
In Midtown a brand-new fire rose
In blood they knew what this would cost
And that's the way the story goes

The city now seemed wide awake
As they saw the rich folk all devoured
A hunger that the rats would slake
Each city street it had been scoured
In working hearts a new strength flowered
Blooming like a winter rose
Death was slow to those high powered
And that's the way the story goes

The peoples' mindset had evolved
No longer were they running scared
Before they had seemed uninvolved
They knew that things could be repaired
As long as they were all prepared
They knew which class they must oppose
This issue had been one that's shared
And that's the way the story goes

Oppression had become profuse
But now there was no bailing out
No guillotine, or gallows noose
The rich knew what this was about

A deal was done they can't back out
From eyes, to claws and twitchy nose
To his tune rats were devout
And that's the way the story goes

The sun it sank beyond the sea
The boy had reached the Mayor's address
And in his house the boy could see
There was one way out of this mess
Too late to solve this game of chess
And now the Mayor will decompose
For soon the rats would gain access
And that's the way the story goes

This was a path none could reverse
And people are now more aware
When music stops the rats disperse
No chance to give in to despair
The final notes hung in the air
Events are drawing to a close
The quiet couldn't be more rare
And that's the way the story goes

If you believe all that you're told
You'll not learn anything brand new
Don't buy the things that you are sold
Don't swallow everything you chew
And watch the things you say and do
Don't suffer greed of CEOs
Make them pay the price that's due
Delay, deny, defend, depose

Princess Goose

A kingdom fair and far away
Where unicorns will never stray
And all the dragons there were slain
Or cast out with so much disdain
Where mortal kings and queens hold sway
In valleys deep and mountains high
You'll find no witches doomed to die

A castle strong and built of stone
Was white and clean like sun-bleached bone
The flags that rose against the blue
Were burgundy and green of hue
Upon the hill it stood alone
In towers that had touched the sky
A princess sat and heaved a sigh

Such a weight her crown became
Each villager had known her name
She could not leave without escorts
Which always left her out of sorts
She hated all the traps of fame
From windows she would watch and spy
And wanted things no gold could buy

This princess by the name Seline
Had now reached the age eighteen
And princes came from far and wide
There was no place that she could hide
To marry she had not been keen
Her parents' law she'd not deny
And frankly she had no reply

Her feet she dragged along the halls
And she avoided many balls
Her hair in bows and dressed in frills
Had left her green about the gills

She would ignore her mother's calls
Her hair trussed up in many pins
With lips pulled back in corpse-like grins

The king and queen would let her choose
A prince that she would soon refuse
He'd wine and dine and feed her praise
Oozing charm with turns of phrase
But all this talk gave her the blues
She'd give them smiles and hold their hand
To her all this was rather bland

No suitor would Seline accept
Her father swore, her mother wept
Perhaps they thought she'd want a bride
There'd be a girl at the next Pride
Seline she had no secret kept
No bride or groom that she desired
For there was no-one she admired

But still she did as she was told
And understood she was controlled
As queen, the laws she must obey
At least for her she had some say
She'd be the price in days of old
A crown can be a heavy weight
When you must find someone to date

Then one day a prince had come
To music of a quiet thrum
His mother stood right by his side
With hopes Seline would be his bride
Seline herself would not succumb
She'd not be swayed by all his charm
Despite the fact he meant no harm

They spoke of places she'd not seen
There was much that she could glean
A happy smile and hollow eyes
More empty than the open skies

The mother had been more than keen
To see her son upon the throne
And have the old king overthrown

Advances cold with no desire
Did not exactly light her fire
For one last time she had declined
The contract never would be signed
But something else would soon transpire
That Seline herself would not forget
And there would be adventure yet

Mountains cold and tipped with snow
More words were spoke and not for show
A witch she was, that mother dear
She had a way to instil fear
The words she spoke, her hands would glow
Magic threads were then set loose
Seline was turned into a goose

Upon the bed Seline would rest
This princess life was truly blessed
But when she woke she got a fright
Something had been changed that night
Perhaps it all had been a test
But feathers, wings, and yellow beak
Confused Seline, she could not speak

At first the royals were not sure
On magic there was no brochure
Seline had honked and flapped her wings
Ensured that she'd knock over things
Her temper now came out so pure
So many theories they would float
And yet the witch had left a note

Her tone was clear and purpose true
It had been something she thought through
In one week hence, you've found no love
This new form will fit like a glove

Deep earth brown and skies of blue
And nothing short of raising hell
The truest love will break the spell

The sun would rise and set three times
And then marked by the church bell chimes
She flapped her wings and honked so loud
Surprised she hadn't drawn a crowd
They understood her frantic mimes
The road was long so she must fly
'Cause if she stayed a goose, she'd die

The king and queen, a bag they'd pack
For there was no looking back
She must find love to then be free
Become who she was meant to be
Seline would have to stay on track
She'd search the land with open heart
And she knew places she could start

The little town beneath the hills
Where rivers slow and then it stills
Upon the wind she swooped and swayed
In the subtle breeze she played
The clean air in her lungs it fills
No sweeter taste than freshest air
For down on ground, she must prepare

The grass was soft beneath webbed feet
Then she waddled down the street
A gentle honk and feathers flapped
For once she wasn't feeling trapped
Seline the goose had felt upbeat
And as she searched each persons' face
She kept her distance just in case

The men who worked in this small town
She had been sure they knew no crown
The women kind they gave her bread
Most too young, too old or wed

Her sprits had been beaten down
This place was sweet but wasn't home
Seline took off and went to roam

The air was cold, no falling rain
As she flew over fields of grain
The sun it sank in shades of green
A storm was here that she'd not seen
The sky was dark and her path was plain
Seline swooped down upon the breeze
To find a sailor on the seas

Towards the ship the Cheeky Swallow
Where in its wake dolphins would follow
And as she had landed on its mast
She thought she'd found her home at last
Sailors prayed to dear Apollo
Overboard this goose they'd toss
For she had been no albatross

They weren't prepared for her sharp bite
She'd not give up without a fight
She managed one or two sharp nips
As she slipped out of all their grips
And swiftly she had taken flight
Towards the shore beneath the moon
She'd have to take a rest quite soon

Seline lay down upon the sand
So tired she could barely stand
Upon her back she'd rest her head
And to the world she was soon dead
It was so nice upon dry land
The sand was warm from this day's heat
But still the spell had not been beat

The morning came and brought the mist
Until midday it would persist
So up she went into the sky
Out in the sun her wings would dry

For moments all plans were dismissed
As Princess Goose had joined the wind
Connections to her old life thinned

Another town not far away
Her hunger there she would allay
The houses small so far below
Deciding then to take it slow
As far above the sky was grey
Over seas a storm had brewed
With shelter she must find some food

Below a barn would be enough
She had not minded sleeping tough
Within its doors she found some hay
The perfect place to end her day
Her goosey wings had had enough
The thunder rolled and with it, rain
Seline would rest her head again

Within the barn some others slept
In stables there some horses kept
They did not mind this silly goose
No noise was made, there was no use
The farm outside was now windswept
And as the night had turned to day
The goose had half a mind to stay

Outside the barn the sky was blue
A brilliant, vibrant, azure hue
She honked her joy and searched for food
Reluctantly she would intrude
She had a hunger that was true
But all she had was scattered seeds
These not enough to meet her needs

The food was fine, not to her taste
She wouldn't let it go to waste
And with her toes she grabbed her bag
The contents made her spirit sag

It was the task that she still placed
Not one crown, not hers alone
For Princess Goose must share the throne

Inside was food, such human things
And hard to eat with goosey wings
But still she tried and dreams returned
She thought of all the princes spurned
Who to tried to buy her love with rings
And through them she could clearly see
But she must wed by crown's decree

Around the farm the cows were fed
Into a shed the sheep were led
Their hair was trimmed for spring was soon
Seline had stayed 'til after noon
A dear sweet hand had thrown her bread
His eyes were dark, his hair was brown
Perhaps his head would fit the crown

She spread her wings and bowed down low
And hoped that he would see and know
But he just grinned and wiped his hand
Then he had the nerve to stand
Before he left more bread he'd throw
Though kindness was enough to rule
Seline knew best she was no fool

With just one loaf her heart was swayed
Her message had not been conveyed
Without her voice had hope been lost?
Did independence have a cost?
She could see now that she had strayed
For no one here had claimed her heart
She must return back to the start

Towards the hills she would return
And mend the bridges left to burn
There was some prince who would be fine
No romance sent by the divine

And though she still had much to learn
It would be best if she went back
And hoped that she could stay on track

Into the sky still clear and bright
She flew on deep into the night
The mountains tall and forests deep
Within the trees she got some sleep
The passing days became a blight
Like rushing wind and changing tide
The time was never on her side

In the night a beast drew near
Too quiet for Seline to hear
And in the dark, its eyes could see
Smelled her there beneath the tree
A twig it cracked, she woke with fear
This feline beast it needed meat
And goose indeed would be a treat

To eat her it was now hell bent
Seline then knew what gooseflesh meant
She spread her wings to appear tall
And oh so loud she gave a call
This noise she made seemed heaven sent
The cat stepped back it had recoiled
It seemed as if its plan was foiled

Then it pounced all teeth and claws
And caught Seline within its jaws
The pain was sharp but she was tough
Just its teeth were not enough
It held her down beneath its paws
She looked it deep into its eyes
And it would now get a surprise

She snapped right back with her sharp beak
Despite her wound she wasn't weak
And as she bit, it jumped away
But then it leaped back in the fray

It gave a hiss and then a squeak
Seline bit back with all her might
She'd not go down without a fight

She bit and scratched, and kicked her feet
But still this cat did not retreat
Her wings had flapped, her honks were loud
Her father would have been so proud
This foe she knew she must defeat
With each lunge, it grew more bold
This horrid beast had kills untold

This princess goose she would be brave
It was her life she'd have to save
There was no prince, no noble knight
And she would live out of pure spite
She'd not go quiet to the grave
Its claws then swung towards her neck
With fury, at its eyes she'd peck

And with a yowl, it scurried back
No longer wanted to attack
Seline stood tall, her eyes ablaze
Remember this she would for days
The night sky still the deepest black
The leaves were scattered on the ground
So she moved on without a sound

Too weak to fly she waddled slow
And watched the fireflies aglow
The wind blew soft, the air was chilled
Though all alone, her heart was filled
There she heard the waters flow
Towards the sound she went to drink
Then into sleep she had to sink

The pond was dark, with stars it gleamed
And it was more than what it seemed
Slowly she then dipped her head
On the surface ripples spread

It was a place of which she'd dreamed
Reflected there, the truth revealed
And something in her soul was healed

Orange beak and feathers white
Looked silver in the pale moonlight
Narcissus never loved this much
And never needed human touch
She then felt strong enough for flight
Into the star filled sky she flew
As the darkness turned to blue

There was no pain, her wounds were small
She crossed the hills and mountains tall
The flags of burgundy and green
The best thing she had ever seen
She flew into the meeting hall
And bowed before the throne of gold
How nice it was to not be cold

There were some gasps of great delight
That she was home from her long flight
A bell was rung and chimed so long
It was enough to draw the throng
This Princess Goose was quite a sight
Blood was still upon her throat
So on her servants moved to dote

The king and queen then showed their face
The townsfolk gave them all their space
Quiet though the bells still chimed
This could not have been better timed
Seline she moved at her own pace
This Princess Goose she did not speak
But had a quill put in her beak

The scraping of her dainty pen
Sounded like a scratching hen
All stood still 'til words were read
Seline herself was filled with dread

The king he had to count to ten
She raised her head and honked her voice
The job was done, she'd made her choice

Those princes who had stayed with hope
Perchance to dream and then elope
Left the hall with heads hung low
With mothers or their dads in tow
Seline was sure that they would cope
Other brides they could secure
Marriage, Seline could not endure

Questions rose about the throne
A goose queen people won't condone
A cry rang out to voice their ire
Seline's bright eyes were filled with fire
Her power came from her alone
This was a claim she would not share
And challenged those who thought to dare

Lightning cracked outside the door
And many dropped onto the floor
The Princess Goose then turned to see
The witch's eyes so filled with glee
The witch declared, "Princess no more!"
And it was then the spell was broke
From in Seline the rage awoke

Her wings spread out, the span was wide
And she had nothing left to hide
The honk she made a crack of thunder
Her self-love tore the spell asunder
The king and queen were by her side
There was wonder in her eyes
And then she grew three times her size

The hall had gasped and then bowed down
This witch had proved herself a clown
Eyes were wide at this strange sight
On steps the king stood at a height

Upon her head he placed a crown
She then spread out a single wing
And wrapped it round the queen and king

The sun it set on this new day
And in the sky the seagulls play
Under flags of red and green
Seline would be the greatest queen
And in this form she chose to stay
With true love that none can reduce
This princess she remained a goose.

2 Tad 2 Vampire Slayer

Damp city streets have a faint neon glow
Little time passed since Tad fought below
He'd no time to train or buy up new blades
But skills with his board, he had those in spades

The nights were bright but no light from the moon
Just magenta and blue across buildings were strewn
The rains had come down and filled up the drains
Cops had come round and locked grates with chains

Here came the rub for Tad and his board
He knew what lived there could not be ignored
And as the nights fell, on the streets he would prowl
Hunting these things, these creatures so foul

His tracks were well worn, he knew them by heart
He had no idea when the horrors would start
The harlots and hookers now knew him by name
Dealers had questions, of what was Tad's game.

So when he was asked what he did every night
He'd exclaim with glee, "My god given right."
His friends would all laugh and then shout again
"It's bad for your health, to stay in the rain."

Tad would skate on towards a new place
To his old apartment he'd not show his face
If the monsters you kill know where you reside
You and your friends will have nowhere to hide

The new place was larger with more room to move
It also showed folks he had nothing to prove
Weapons of steel, of iron, and wood,
Could be seen on the walls wherever you stood

His board by the door, all shiny and new
And a wide eastern window with a breath-taking view

The dark city glowed and sparkled with light
The sun rose up sharply, burning so bright

His job was in tech, security codes
Privacy, secrets, as freedom corrodes
And while their lives were now strictly surveilled
In finding these creatures, so far, he had failed

Each day at his desk he watched through his screen
All streets lit up in magenta and green
Then in the night he'd search for a trace
Of black eyes and fangs in a horrid white face

He went to a church, and stayed for a while
A priest passed him by as he walked down the aisle
And Tad asked of things the Priest had not heard
To priests, these dark things had never occurred

Tad then explained of his skills and his curse
The priest remained calm, but his tone was terse
"A promise can be a hard thing to keep."
Tad understood, but his time wasn't cheap

He flat out explained of what he desired
And then made a list of what was required
The priest gave a smirk and then he indulged
And promised these things would not be divulged

A largish knife blessed, of silver 'twas made
As sharp as a tooth and of highest grade
Had bottles and vials of water so pure
Twice was distilled and holy for sure

Then on a whim the priest blessed his board
It was now a tool of the almighty lord
Tad gave a smirk and then a small shrug
Pulling this man into a tight hug

The priest had offered to join in this quest
Promised to do twice his very best

His offer was empty, knew Tad would decline
This man wouldn't put his neck on the line

Tad played the game and considered the deal
Knowing the truth that it wasn't real
Tad then said no for his age and his strength
And he was talking in ad nauseum length

So he gathered these gifts and left at a run
Checking that he still carried his gun
The night was lit up like fire and ice
He ignored bright signs to sell and entice

Some said of Tad, he's a liar who cheats
He didn't find things below the dark streets
No bloodbath of danger down in the dark deep
There was never a reason to lose any sleep

In their heart of hearts they silently knew
Evil lurked between magenta and blue
Posters with names of those who were lost
Tad knew for sure whose paths they had crossed

On his nightly route, he looked for a sign
A signal of weirdness, perhaps the divine
He checked in with those he had known by name
But the well trodden path looked much the same

One horrid night, there was one missing face
She was not in her usual place
A young cheerful girl who walked in the lights
And had owning a bar right there in her sights

Kat worked in a club and slept in her van
It was an upgrade from the beat-up sedan
She was smart as a whip and a very good friend
He hoped he'd would find her around the next bend

He then took a turn, on an old rusted grate
A snarl of her hair was left there as bait

S Jayne Bradley

He knew it was hers by the colour and tone
And then on the ground, her cellular phone

Tad's heart racing fast, the grate he then lifted
Up from the dark the smell of blood drifted
He scooped up his board and slipped down the hole
Became one with the shadows and blind as a mole

The water it dripped, and the smell was unique
From out of the darkness, he heard a faint shriek
It was a low sound so distant and small
Deliberate movements had slowed to a crawl

The water had reached way beyond his guts
To go any further was certainly nuts
The air had a chill that clawed at his chest
As his body slowed, for time he was pressed

A few gasps of air and then he would swim
The drain was so cold, and the light was too dim
Tad knew he must find another way down
If he carried on, he'd certainly drown

The surface was still; no cars passing by
Only the sound of the rain from the sky
He pulled out his map of the tunnels below
With a finger he traced the path he might go

Half drenched in shit and soaked to the bone
He ran three streets down, and still all alone
He passed sewer grates and an open storm drain
To subway stairs now blocked with a chain

And under the fence, it wasn't too hard
Trouble was near, so he was on his guard
He rolled down the stairs, and clacked over cracks
Soon he was standing before the old tracks

Graffiti still lined the greying white walls
Papers they floated 'round kiosks and stalls

The Knight Witch

The past here still lingered, refusing to die
Tad took a moment to breathe and to sigh

Then with a rumble, the roar of the train
Kicked all his thoughts straight out of his brain
The train thundered past with eyes bright as fire
Tad jumped back like he touched a live wire

Taking a tumble right onto his ass
As strange blurry faces pressed up at the glass
A bright shooting pain rung in his head
Into the darkness the subway train sped

The silence was thick and filled up his brain
 He took a deep breath to keep himself sane
He dragged himself up and moved with intent
With a shake of his limbs, he began his descent

Onto the tracks, he then grabbed his board
Held it outstretched like it was a sword
He turned on the torch as he strained his ears
Using the light to assuage his fears

The rain water dripped and fell with a splash
And far up ahead he heard a door crash
Tad paused in his tracks and stayed very still
He held a deep breath; he needed to chill

Then in a flash, he quickened his pace
It now was his turn to take up the chase
Sure Kat was here, and he hoped she'd not turned
Or she would be dead, and he'd have her burned

A maintenance door was bent on the tracks
It looked like it had been hit with an axe
He lowered his board and picked up the door
It wouldn't be hit by the train anymore

The opening revealed a long flight of stairs
It went to a place where they once did repairs

Tad gave a sniff and he knew that scent well
This place was a definite gateway to hell

The thickness of flesh left to decompose
It certainly wasn't the smell of a rose
Foetid wet air now clung to his skin
It stuck in his throat and made his head spin

Downstairs he trudged, his board at his hip
And still up above he heard the pipes drip
A room lit with blue, it hummed and it glowed
He knew from this place electricity flowed

Inside of the room a headless corpse laid
Across a blank wall dark blood had been sprayed
There was no one else, from what he could see
These rooms always had just one attendee

He then left the room, and followed the trail
And put his board down, and opened the sail
He rolled down the hall towards a stone gate
Now all of his chances would be up to fate

As he breathed in the air, the smell was much worse
And under his breath he let out a curse
The tunnel was smooth, so he could still ride
Down this dark road on his board he would glide

The tunnel was filled with the sound of his wheels
His balance unsteady, his weight on his heels
Abruptly he found the end of the road
Tad clutched his board, to the edge he then strode

No heavier silence had anyone known
And onto the ground, himself he had thrown
Over the edge he hoped they'd not seen
But he saw the lights, magenta and green

A necropolis stood under pale lights
Faintly they glowed in yellows and whites

The Knight Witch

Tunnels and walls had been carved out of stone
Some sections made out of discarded bone

So many creatures and none of them stilled
If just one had seen, poor Tad would be killed
Then through the dark came a harrowing scream
Piercing and sharp, wrenched from Tad's worst dream

Tad swore the voice was the Kat that he knew
She was alive, so he had to come through
He had to climb down, he could not delay
Around him he searched for a much better way

The pathways were thin; the stairways were steep
They twisted in darkness and led him down deep
A mist hung about his ankles and shoes
Empty streets twisted, which way he must choose

His breathing was soft, he'd not make a noise
And he walked the path with balance and poise
A shadow of this vile place he became
Soon every foul monster would know his name

Eyes from high windows had not seen him yet
It wasn't the time to panic or fret
Towers stood tall in pale misty light
The darkness enough to stay out of sight

Somewhere up high a flock of bats shrieked
Far up above their flapping forms streaked
He'd not seen them close and just heard their cries
Staying quiet and hidden in case they were spies

Who knew that deep down and under the roads
There was such a place not reliant on codes?
Just flickers of light in magenta and green
And towers of darkness with monsters' unseen

Following the sound that Kat had just made
Tad lowered his board and pulled out his blade

He did have a gun, that too at the ready
His aiming was fine if he could stay steady

Down alleys he rolled, the sound like a hum
As he scoured the streets, his heart like a drum
The rhythm that beat was hard in his ears
And through open doors and windows he peers

Then with a jolt, he met someone's gaze
This creature hissed, its bright eyes ablaze
Tad staggered back and tripped on his board
The creature emerged to claim its reward

Tad sliced with his blade, its fingers were slashed
Recoiling in pain, the monster then dashed
He wanted to kill and never to maim
Tad swung with this knife and had perfect aim

It fell with a crack and Tad heaved a sigh
He was relieved and that wasn't a lie
Tad took a quick glance and was filled with fright
Something else moved in the misty light

Before any more of them could perceive
He stashed his blessed blade right down his left sleeve
His gun on his hip was still at his side
A small laser gun that had been his pride

From the deep shadows, there came a harsh screech
Out of Tad's head went his powers of speech
The vampires scrambled and moved like a cat
With their jagged mouths, they hissed, and they spat

Too many had grabbed him and dragged him away
Their numbers and strength meant he was now prey
Now at the mercy of this rabid horde
They lifted him high and carried his board

Into a place with a roof that was high
The sort of place where the breeze goes to die

The Knight Witch

There on a dais, he saw an old man
White as a ghost, he so needed a tan

His cold, bloody eyes met with Tad's own
In this cursed place, Tad was all alone
The long-fingered hand grasped at his face
Its movements like liquid, with power and grace

His voice was a whisper with barely a hiss
Tad strained to see more in this dark abyss
Behind him he heard them cackle and shriek
The creature he gestured for silence to speak

"The first human here out of his own choice,
Perhaps we all here should dance and rejoice,"
The malice was clear on his bloodless lips
His smile was sick, like a partial eclipse

"Such a strange thing to have by your side"
He held out the board, then Tad replied
"Monster of Monsters in this foul domain,
Why do you dwell down here in the drain?"

His thin lips twisted and curled to a sneer
Tad then calmed his soul, let go of his fear
"You ask why I came, and not cause my death
I thought I'd be dead before I drew breath,"

This monster then called for all to let go
Curious still his children moved slow
Tad regained his feet, his gun was now taken
Staring him down was leaving Tad shaken

The vampire grinned his misshapen smile
Tad understood he was in denial
Whether or not he lived or he died
Would be based upon the time he could bide

If he was to see a new light of day
There were many games he needed to play

Tad knew if he could just reclaim his board
He could then escape this vampire horde

The darkness was thick, but he could see his skin
And he felt the horror that oozed from within
A cry then rang out diverting his mind
The girl, she still lived! Soon Kat he must find

The vampire's face turned up, his eyes now closed
He had no idea of the danger Tad posed
Up his left sleeve where he had hidden his knife
To only be used to save his own life

He drew out the blade as quick as a flash
And swinging it wide, he gave him a slash
The monster recoiled and exposed his jaws
His fingertips grew from nails into claws

The board had been dropped, it fell with a clack
Tad then surprised with a second attack
Behind him he heard the other things howl
The sound and their breath revoltingly foul

He picked up his board, and unfolded the sail
Rushed towards the beast, aiming to impale
The thing stepped aside with a tired old smile
The breath from his mouth was putrid and vile

Tad scurried on past, a wide grin on his face
This vampire bitch would have to give chase
Wheels then hit stone, and he took off at speed
With vampires behind, he had taken the lead

The claws on the stone, they echoed around
Then down by Tad's feet a passage he found
The door barely seen there deep in the black
He tucked himself down with his board on his back

The sounds from outside soon became dead
And then this brave slayer now had a clear head

The passage turned up to a higher floor
To get himself out, he kicked, and he swore

Tad tumbled out hard, all battered and bruised
He stretched out his bones still somewhat amused
The room was so silent, no sound had been made
A cry from his friend crashed like a cascade

"Kat?" He called out, and at first no reply
"I hope you are here, I'm not gonna lie,"
A small whimpered sob and a rattle of chains
"You would leave me here, if you had any brains,"

"Doubtful," he said and with a wry smile
"If you won't escape, I'll stay for a while,"
He then sauntered up to where she now lay
Knowing soon he'd have to keep monsters at bay

Her eyes had been bound, her hands had been tied
He had to get close and stay by her side
Her pretty red lips, the palest of skin
The marks on her neck showed a monster within

The bruises were dark, and all over the place
And Tad he could see the pain in her face
He reached out a hand and poor Kat recoiled
Then at her chains he worried and toiled

They rattled and clunked but did not come apart
Tad had known they'd be trouble right from the start
The ropes at her wrist had now been untied
As she could have done if she had just tried

She grabbed at his arm with a cold clammy hand
For a moment poor Tad did not understand
He tried so much harder to set the girl free
Distracted by fear he just did not see

The chain was too strong, the steel would not break
And Kat stared at him as if he were steak

"Do not set me free, or we will both die"
Her words had cracked as she started to cry

He then saw her fangs and looked at her face
Kat did not belong here in this place
"I'm so sorry my child, you will have to run."
That's when the mask on her face came undone

"Too good to be true," he grumbled and muttered
And hoped those weren't the last words he uttered
Now something else sat and spoke in Kat's place
He scooped up his board, it laughed in his face

If Kat was alive, she'd be somewhere up high
A tower, a folly, a place where bats fly
Towards a small window he looked to the west
This place was a maze and surely a test

In this room he saw a tall winding stair
That led deeper into the vampires' lair
So as fake Kat laughed, he slashed at her throat
Black blood sprayed out, this devil he smote

He rushed up the stairs without any sound
Hoping and praying that he'd not be found
And down far below he heard the king's call
And hoped that his grief was enough of a stall

At the top of the tower, a bridge to the next
This maze of a building was leaving him vexed
He looked all around at the chasms below
This leg of the journey he'd have to take slow

Out of the tower, a bunch of bats flew
A great search for Tad he knew would ensue
Beside this thin bridge he paused for a spell
How long he should wait, poor Tad could not tell

He watched up above and the stairs close behind
Then spotted a tower where one small light shined

The Knight Witch

In his heart of hearts far deep in his soul
That tiny light, Tad now knew was his goal

The bridge it was crumbing and horridly old
Tad wasn't sure if for him it would hold
But this was the path he knew he must take
Under his feet the stone started to shake

All worries escaped right out of his head
As over the bridge on his board he sped
For a second he thought he heard the stone crack
The sound chilled his bones, but he wouldn't look back

The threshold was crossed of the second tower
It took a few seconds but seemed like an hour
He settled his breath and then turned around
The thin bridge collapsed with a thunderous sound

A sigh of relief as he started to move
In a whispered thought, "I'm finding my groove,"
The stairs leading down were open and wide
Tad softly mumbled, "This will be a ride,"

He lined up his board upon the first stair
Excited to feel the wind in his hair
Before he let go he counted to five
And hoped at the end he'd still be alive

Rolling down stairs was not his first time
Like riding the waves, just not as sublime
The board it then rolled and time seemed to slow
Behind him two eyes in a fiery glow

A pale hand grasped for the back of his shirt
With a burst of speed, he escaped unhurt
Now out of its reach as the board picked up speed
Tad was rather relieved he'd not have to bleed

Each step was a thump that changed to a rumble
The speed that he moved he'd have to stay humble

For if he had thought that great he would be
The stone it would take him just like the sea

So he rolled with the punches and let himself flow
For the board showed no signs it was going to slow
The thunderous rumble was more than skin deep
Tad knew down below he'd fall in a heap

The tower stairs twisted, he suffered each turn
Yet still in his mind he could see those eyes burn
Soon he had landed and still on his feet
One second later he was on the street

No sunlight was waiting, no growing day
The misty white glow not going away,
He searched for the tower, one with the light
He saw the faint glow was not within sight

Maintaining his speed, in that direction
He rolled that way with little correction
The tower was tall, a castle below
Was Kat inside? Poor Tad couldn't know

Tad checked his knife, with blood it was stained
And looked at the window; his colour drained
This was the time he could choose to turn back
Could leave her behind, abandon the black?

But he knew he could not leave her down here
Despite all his anger, frustration and fear
She was his friend and she'd do the same
This was both their lives, this wasn't a game

The castle before him was vast in its size
A spire above him was where his fate lies
The sparkle of light he hoped was his friend
And up to that spire he'd have to ascend

A large stony wall surrounded this place
Huge iron spikes thrust out at its base

The Knight Witch

Black metal spears poked out from the top
At least for a moment intruders would stop

With his strength renewed, he rolled to the gate
Going through here it was tempting fate
Pulling on chains, a portcullis came down
Cutting him off from the rest of the town

The castle was still with the creatures outside
They wandered the streets, they shouted and cried
The sound of their voices had given him pause
They reached between bars with fingers and claws

Now safe behind the barred gate he'd locked
He reached to his hip where his gun was cocked
But it was not there, the gun had been snatched!
Crafty Tad grinned and a new plan was hatched

Hissing and crying, and deep guttural moans
The sounds of them chilled him down to his bones
There in the doorways and windows now cracked
For him three were waiting before they attacked

Time it was ticking and Tad couldn't tarry
His board and his knife were all he could carry
There were just the three that stood in his way
With all of his might he would make them pay

He held out his blade and called them to fight
For a second they paused with Tad in their sight
Instead of the knife, he rushed with his board
Harder and stronger than any old sword

With his speed and his strength swinging so hard
The first one he hit was one that he scarred
Black hair was long and framing its face
Deep set blue eyes, and Tad it would trace

The other two watched and waited to see
Which of them would the last one standing be

Tad swung again but the movement was blocked
The board clattered down in combat now locked

He took a step forward struck with his blade
This blood sucking fiend he vowed to degrade
The knife broke its skin, but no blood did ooze
Its heart did not beat, its skin didn't bruise

So, he took a leap, with more strength than faith
Stabbed this holy blade in the neck of the wraith
From his pocket he pulled the water once blessed
And splashed it onto the vampire's chest

It howled out its rage then crumpled to dust
The others looked on with fear and disgust
The palest of skin with veins underneath
Their lips were pulled back, revealing their teeth

Tad raised a finger across his own throat
Implied that the others were in the same boat
Towards them he lunged his blade tightly held
He moved with such speed, soon the others were felled

With movements so swift with water he splashed
Then with his knife he cut and he slashed
Because of his speed he'd caught them off guard
The blessings soon left these vampires charred

Three mounds of dust now lay far behind
And there was more trouble for him to still find
So up flights of stairs in a darkened maze
Tad hoped in that window the light still ablaze

The tower was narrow and reached greater heights
The stairs were so many, he lost count of flights
As he reached higher floors, he saw a faint glow
The chill in the air had caused him to slow

Tad took a deep breath and stepped in the room
Here in this place he courted his doom

The Knight Witch

The space it was dim, but he could still see
Kat! She survived! Now his friend he would free

Kat looked at Tad with those eyes that he knew
Dark and familiar, they sparkled like dew
He checked out her neck to find a fresh bite
But he could not tell, and not in this light

The windows were barred, there was no escape
Behind him he heard the swish of a cape
A hand on his back, the one exit closed
And to this foul beast his neck was exposed

Tad spun around his heart in his chest
The fear in his eyes was clearly expressed
Nightmares and horrors within hollow eyes
This notion of death it would galvanise

Behind him Kat screamed, the sound like a blade
It cut through his soul and then wouldn't fade
The King of the Vampires grinned teeth and all
Tad braced himself, prepared for a brawl

But that never came, the vampire spoke,
His voice not a whisper, but barely a croak
"You think I don't know what things you have seen
You've trodden the path of the foul and unclean,"

Tad took a step back, and glanced once at Kat
He wished that he had his gun or a bat
"I know what you did, our blood you have spilled
How many of mine own kindred you've killed,"

"Your death will be slow, that is assured,
And into this place, I have had you lured,"
The noise from below now rose like a tide
The creature then knew Tad's death was denied,

Hollars and hoots and calls of Tad's name
Some voices he knew, and some by acclaim

A feeling of warmth then ran up his spine
For a moment he dreamed it all would be fine

And confidence came and gave him a boost
So many concerns had now been reduced
He heard them; the harlots, the homeless as well
Had come to the place where vampires dwell

The relief that he felt was tinged with his fear
He hadn't desired for them to come here
To fight all the monsters from down underneath
But he knew that they would be armed to the teeth

For a moment he breathed, the monster then lunged
Into the darkness the tower had plunged
Tad felt his claws strike deep in his skin
Into his navel, his chest, and his chin

His voice had been lost to the tumult below
The strength of their voices made his soul glow
Deep in the shadows, he let despair reign
But good friends had found him down in the drain

And then to his right he heard a chain snap
Something had broken within this sprung trap
The sound it had given the vampire pause
Tad shuffled back away from his claws

The board still in reach and though he was weak
He thought of the havoc his prone form could wreak
The rattle of steel and grunts of a fight
Because of the dark just out of Tad's sight

Assumed it was Kat, she must have been turned
His friend to the surface she'd not be returned
The board he swung out, as wild as he could
As blind as a bat, his aim wasn't good

The danger was real and so close to doom
A light flickered on and lit up the room

The Knight Witch

Kat was now up and light on her feet
And there stood the priest, no longer dressed neat

Alive in the shadows, the Vampire King
It looked like his wounds were starting to sting
Tad tried to stand, but felt himself slip
Then Kat and the priest had him in their grip

But with all the strength this man could muster
His next attack was one that had lustre
He lowered his board and then took the plunge
From this existence this fiend he'd expunge

Tad's hands dug in deep, he cursed and he swore
He was exhausted right down to his core
And black blood oozed out, in places it sprayed
Tad's mental health was now certainly frayed

He stood up once more with blood on his shirt
The wounds on his chest were bleeding and hurt
From poor Tad, Kat had stepped back away
The priest saw the wounds and started to pray

The old priest reached out and then held Tad's arm
And Tad turned to Kat with fear and alarm
She opened her mouth with her teeth on display
Despite the bad light, she hadn't turned grey

Tad took the head of the Vampire king
Up to the surface they would take that thing
Down the long stairs to the base of the tower
And far down below the air had turned sour

Flickering torches revealed who was there
Many had gathered below in the square
A cry then went out and Tad raised his fist
Their joy and their grief would always persist

A calm it took over the crowd and the dead
And many deep thoughts had run through Tad's head

This vampiric curse would have to be broken
And all understood this fact was unspoken

Tad cheered them on as each corner they'd search
And cleansed with water the priest had at church
They blessed all the walls, so they'd never thrive
There would be no vampire here left alive

Most bodies were left in heaps to decay
Some people stood over the corpses to pray
Tad had his wounds checked over and cleaned
There were lots of scratches from that awful fiend

There were other scars on his chest that had healed
Of surgeries past from lives not revealed
 Tad stood up straight, his strength now renewed
And into his plan the others were clued

He took the king's head and led them all out
The route they followed was all round-about
Taking odd paths and opening doors
Pausing to make holes in the old wooden floors

Each passage made had left no place to hide
Rooms were thrown open and doors they flung wide
All paths had been mapped and tunnels were traced
No spot was left out, not even in haste

First to the room where controls had been found
And push the right buttons all shiny and round
So that down below would light up with white
And if any remained, they'd have no will to fight

They booted the servers and brought them online
And in that dark city a new light would shine
The cheers rung out loud, but no-one dared stay
If the monsters came back, there'd be hell to pay

Then Tad explained they should go back home
Stay off the streets, no more they could roam

The Knight Witch

He urged them to stay where it was the brightest
No-one should stray, no, not in the slightest

He remembered their names and faces as well
Those who for him would walk through all hell
For a moment would come when he'd call them back
Into new danger, down deep in the black

Tad's next task was to pass on his prize
To those up above who had closed their eyes
They had never seen the monsters arrive
Nor did they care if some didn't survive

The blood wasn't theirs, not drawn by their hand
And now it was time for that line in the sand
He rolled to the stairs of the great city hall
And no-one had noticed he was there at all

Out of a bag he dropped the foul head
The hollow eyes staring now vacant and dead
Tad showed the fangs, on the stairs it was placed
Its hateful visage could not be erased

The fat cats would see and they would soon learn
That things must be done or the city would burn
Tad knew that he might be the one with the match
He'd let the smoke rise as the city would catch

As he turned his back and then left unseen
The city was bright in magenta and green
Above in the streets, it was a new day
And now no more monsters here left to slay

His work was not done, not by half a mile
He'd be doing this work for more than a while
Tad wandered back home and dreamed of the sea
But in neon streets, he was meant to be

He walked his old haunts and checked on the grates
He was greeted by all of his best mates

They spoke of their deeds and the old rotting head
And of some reactions, so little was said

New laws were passed but not much was done
Just one or two people now carried a gun
Tad walked his route, no movements concealed
Many more hunters now out in the field

Times had not changed, just got harder to hide
And Tad had his board and he would still ride
He searched down the alleys for all escapees
The city was cleansed with far too much ease

Kat had been fine and went back to her van
To live some kind of life the best that she can
Tad would stop by and have a small talk
Sometimes they would even go for a walk

It was at that time, he decided to leave
The city was safe, no more could he grieve
The ocean had called, he wasn't the same
A vampire slayer with no fame to claim

He missed the bright seas, the sparkle of spray
And, most of all, he just wanted the day
A city of darkness, magenta and green
No longer held monsters that travelled unseen

Tad packed his things, prepared to depart
Though the people who saved him would keep his heart
A knock on the door had seemed rather rude
He supposed then a friend would lighten his mood

Tad opened the door and to his surprise
A thing stared back from dark, hollow eyes
It grinned with its fangs so bright on display
"For the damage you've done, I will make you pay,"

But Tad was too quick, out the window he sailed
His board in his hand, his luck had prevailed

The Knight Witch

He hit the ground hard, and rattled his bones
The creature it shrieked in such dulcet tones

Tad smiled wide, a new game had started
And he was so pleased he hadn't departed
All bets were off, the hunt was now on
Not all of the vampire kindred were gone

He skated down alleys, alerted his friends
This isn't the place where this story ends
Light up a candle even if you don't pray
For Tad now has even more vampires to slay

S Jayne Bradley

The Pirate and his Paramour

The water's deep beside the keep
Where pirates' wives will kneel and weep
Their heads hang low, the pirates high
These privateers were doomed to die

They wore their flags of bears and stags
Were dressed up fine in rotted rags
The hangman walked to beating drums
A lady sat upon her thumbs

Her hair of gold was bought and sold
To hide the fact she'd gotten old
Her face was white just like a sail
Her beauty seemed beyond the pale

No crowned head, her husband dead
He had been murdered in his bed
The son had mourned, the mother cried
But this, of course, just meant she lied

Her colours bright, she ruled the night
The other lords came out of spite
With open throats, to peace induce
All those involved had called a truce

And of her claim, of land and name
The war of rule, it never came
Agreements made, the fist was stayed
The hardest game they ever played

So dressed in green she had been seen
Acting like she was a queen
There was no claim, no family line
Her blue blood might as well be brine

She raised her son, by sword and gun
Her power would not be undone

Death, it came, no door was blocked
So many plans she could concoct

She was no queen, no princess sweet
She craved the blood of peasant meat
The working class, they knew first hand
That death she held within her hand

Her son was kind, a sharpish mind
The nicest man you'd ever find
He grew up tall, he grew up proud
And never shared his thoughts aloud

In bondage held, his spirit quelled
Despite the fact, his anger swelled
There was a tide behind his wall
He craved to see his mother fall

So dressed in style, sweetly he'd smile
But his own throat was filled with bile
He played her games, obeyed her still
And hoped and prayed to find free will

The years went by, how time would fly
The boy, now man, would still comply
He toed the line, and bowed his head
But each lived day was filled with dread

Then one night, without a fight
She let her son out of her sight
A bride he'd want, to wed one day
And make sure heirs were on the way

She was quite sure that he was pure
And he'd find a wife who was demure
It was a ball, of higher class
Who served in crystal, not in glass

So in he went with civet scent
And dressed so well for this event

He danced and ate, and drank his fill
Tomorrow he'd be feeling ill

He knew each face and trim of lace
There was no person out of place
But then he'd seen, across the floor
A stranger enter through the door

His beard was dark, the contrast stark
His cold eyes like those of a shark
They were no queen or princess cute
He was a man of ill repute

The son was fair, his golden hair
Was drawing an intriguing stare
The young man gazed, and he was keen
This man was unlike all he'd seen

His clothes were black, and on his back
A sword that was meant for attack
The guards had seen, the shiny blade
A rule it had been disobeyed

He drew the sword, expression bored,
Relinquished like a fancy lord
The man then bowed, "My name is Jack,
You bet your ass I want it back,"

He stalked inside, nothing to hide
His shoulders back and filled with pride
His crew gave chase, no weapons seen
Compared to guests they were unclean

With no disguise, the captain's eyes
They opened wider with surprise
The prince had seen something brand new
It was a light he'd not eschew

Then in a daze, his heart ablaze
He had returned the stranger's gaze

The captain smiled and then drew near
He downed his wine to quell his fear

They touched their hands, and talked of sands
In distant and exotic lands
The night passed on, and still they spoke
Shielded by the stranger's cloak

They played no game, each gave their name
For it was love they'd soon proclaim
Ol' Captain Jack, and young Prince Flynn
They knew their time was wearing thin

They did not dance, but shared a kiss
There was no better ball than this
So then they planned that they would flee
And join Jack's crew upon the sea

So on the night the two took flight
And planned to leave before the light
The air was cold, and fog rolled in
Yet sweat was pouring off their skin

They saw the boat, 'twas still afloat
But Flynn felt something at his throat
The prince then turned to see the guard
His escape it had been barred

Captain Jack did not look back
He hoped that Flynn would cut him slack
For pirates in this port were hung
He had to go before traps sprung

So Flynn returned, his heart was spurned
And he avowed all bridges burned
His mother claimed he'd not be free
She would select his bride to be

So, time it went, 'twas poorly spent
Out of shape Flynn's mum was bent

He never wed, no princess bride
For him all of her tears had dried

Life of leisure, built on pleasure
To her standards he'd not measure
He broke her grip and gave her pains
Until she had to drop his reigns

But still he stayed, with debts from trade
His status here would now degrade
So off to sea, from shore to shore
Pretending that he wasn't poor

Against the tide, without a guide
Independence was a point of pride
He earned some wounds and gained some scars
From burly men in seedy bars

The Captain Jack was feeling slack
For guilt he had upon his back
He changed his ship, and got new crew
And into booze his life he threw

This pirate man, without a plan
Was more than just a hatchet man
An invite came, the grandest ball
He'd dress up nice and heed the call

The doctor said, "What's in his head?"
A trap could mean they end up dead
A reckless thought, and need for cash
Had Captain Jack start acting rash

The blonde first mate was filled with hate
He did not know how to debate
A surly maid, who held her blade
She knew most of a sailor's trade

The doctor came, and with his aim
He made most marksmen feel their shame

The Knight Witch

The Captain's Crew were not that bright
But always eager for a fight

So with his crew, they planned things through
And headed out with much ado
Dressed up nice, it felt quite weird
Things got worse as the date neared

All eyes stared, and teeth were bared
The Captain thought that no one cared
This port was clean, and showed him grace
Even if they knew his face

So through the door, across the floor
They weren't in hiding anymore
There were no masks, no false pretence
The atmosphere was somewhat tense

The group spread out, would give a shout
With their clients' whereabouts
An invite came and offered work
The party was indeed a perk

From stem to stern, the crew would learn
What job this was and what they'd earn
They'd have their hands upon this prize
Before the next day's sun will rise

The Captain saw, with sagging jaw,
A face that stuck deep in his craw
Those golden locks, eyes like the sea
He thought at once it couldn't be

Of all the isles, in many miles
He'd never thought he'd face these trials
A racing heart, a grinning face
The Captain was now giving chase

The man drew near, his face was clear
And Cupid struck him with a spear

Flynn then bowed low, a simple tilt
His hand had snaked towards his hilt

Though hands restrained, the Captain pained
From his face all colour drained
The Captain stood, with chest thrust out
Within his eyes he carried doubt

"My Captain fine, you crossed a line,
You left me to the guards, you swine!"
The Captain bowed, so deep indeed,
Offered up his neck to bleed.

"The seas are cruel, I am a fool,
And you remain a precious jewel,"
His cheeks had flushed, the sweetest pink
Flynn had little time to think.

The Captain beamed, and like he dreamed
He knew that he could be redeemed
"The Lady Queen, she must have passed
To find you in my midst at last,"

"My mother dear, she lives I fear,
But she knows not that I am here,"
As two hands clasped, they moved to dance
Enjoyed the meeting made by chance

And at this time, the crew did mime,
That they had organized their crime
They waved their arms and called his name
He ignored them for this old flame

His hands were tied, his crew decried
They couldn't free him if they tried
Sparkling lights, both men enthralled
The crew was standing there appalled

With bow and kiss and promised bliss
Flynn had said they'd reminisce

The Knight Witch

Aboard the ship, they'd spend the night
Start the job when stars were right

The Doctor man, he hatched a plan
Approached young Flynn, his face deadpan
A gift he gave so they could track
In case the prince did not come back

So with one hand, he left a brand
Like he'd made markings in the sand
For a few days, the crew would see
Exactly where the prince would be

Then with much pain, and strong disdain
The crew regaled the job again:
A bandit crew dwelled in the woods
Had stolen wives and hard-earned goods

Their boss had killed, and he was thrilled
To do the crimes that he had willed
The stolen gold, would line his purse
Made promises of doing worse.

Thus was described, the crew had jibed
That they could win if he was bribed
A man built broad, and badly scarred
They were remaining on their guard

The captain sat and clutched his hat
His brain danced like an acrobat
So quick it moved without restraint
The pictures that his brain did paint!

The night was dead and, on his bed
The Captain's anger had been fed
A promise made had not been kept
His rage so strong he hadn't wept

He went to sleep and mad he'd steep
The wine he drank had not been cheap

His head would ache, and he'd regret
That he had needs that were not met

When dawn had come, he had felt dumb
These feelings he would overcome
No broken heart would stop his quest
He'd hold this grief close to his chest

The dice were thrown and overblown
His heart hurt like a kidney stone
So, focus came to dull the pain
The words he spoke were quite profane

His crew in tow, they'd find their foe
But they knew things he did not know
They walked the road with eyes so wide
This was a game of seek and hide

The road was dirt, they were alert
To stop the risk of getting hurt
The woods were thick, and shadows deep
Around the trees the vines would creep

The Doctor knew, as did the crew
What they'd be walking right into
So late that night, they told Ol' Jack
The prince may not be coming back

The captain's rage they could not gage
He did not free it from its cage
So resolute and calm of face
All he did was change the pace

They did not rest, onwards they pressed
The Captain now a man possessed
Though in his heart he did not know
If Flynn was either friend or foe

For this affair, they moved with care
As they approached the bandit's lair

The Knight Witch

The noise was loud, and they could see
The lordly Flynn on bended knee

The Captain saw with hanging jaw
With pity his cold heart did thaw
Flynn was restrained and beaten hard
And had been chained up in the yard

The camp it stood within the wood,
Most went without a mask or hood
Their weapons sharp, they clenched their fists
No tougher bandit clan exists

And they moved west, at his request
The Captain's words were from his chest
"A plan we have, surround them all
Then sally forth upon my call"

The crew agreed to do the deed
For him they were prepared to bleed
The goal was clear, with blades in hand
They were about to make their stand

There was a plan, shit hit the fan
With swords held high the fight began
They struck first blows, but not one died
Although surprise was on their side

As hits rang out, poor Flynn did shout
And called for them to get him out
He pulled his chains, and called for Jack
"My Captain, will you take me back?"

To their lament, out of a tent
There came the king with ill intent
He raised his blade, this Bandit King
And moved just like a coiled spring

His hair was blond, his eyes of ice
The Captain feared he'd pay a price

His sword aloft, he calmed his fear
To save the one that he held dear

With clashing steel, it was surreal
That Jack had fought with so much zeal
Each step was made just like a dance
He left no move or strike to chance

The crew they fought, as they were taught
"Just fight until you're dead or caught"
These bandit brutes, fought for acclaim
The Doctor just had better aim

The lady sweet, quick on her feet,
Carved bandits like they were fresh meat
He smashed in skulls, the blonde-haired thug
And let them drop while looking smug

The fight was long, their foes were strong
They thought it wouldn't take this long
But they held on, and more were killed
Soon their quest would be fulfilled

The Captain's hand, in gesture grand
Informed the crew of what he'd planned
To break the chains, and snap the rope
And give this ailing prince some hope

The Doctor rushed, his tone was hushed
And Flynn he spoke but then was shushed
The Doctor tried, failed more than twice
One broken chain would not suffice

The ropes were tight, deep they did bite
And Flynn could only look contrite
The doctor stood, and Flynn was free
But still he sat on bended knee

The Captain swore, fought like a boar
Through bandit flesh his sabre tore

"Get up and fight," the Captain cried
Relieved that Flynn, he hadn't died

The Captain's word, it had been heard
But this request it seemed absurd
Still in the dirt, Flynn lay there hurt
His tone was frayed and rather curt

"You fool, I bleed! Your help I need,"
Less complaint and more he'd plead
Flynn could not brawl, he had no strength
No voice to argue this at length

So on they'd fight, before the night
Each villain dead or out of sight
The Bandit foe, they took his head
Left the rest in piles of dead

The gold they stole, it was their goal
But soon the Captain took control
He called them back for all their loot
They dropped it all before his boot

Then Flynn did stand, and reached a hand
Hoping to say goodbye to land
The Captain bowed and Flynn had swooned,
 Despite the dangers of his wound

The woods were clear, they had no fear
And all now had what they held dear
Then to the town, to claim their prize
To look their client in the eyes

The noble lord, he held his sword
Declined to give them their reward
But three more blades and just one gun
Negotiations were then done

There was more gold than they could hold
Towards the ship in barrels rolled

They sang their tunes as dawn arose
As fluid as the river flows

A moment blessed, there was a test
For the Captain and his guest
The ocean there, it would await
For now they would complete their date

The wine they drank, in bed they sank
They only had themselves to thank
Their hearts entwined, a night was shared
And on Jack's ship both souls were bared

The sun did set, and in the trees
They told some stories such as these
By candle light, or fire's blaze
Some talked of past and better days

On winter's nights, when stars are lights
They talk of pirates and their fights
A price was paid, the foes had lost
Bandits paid the steepest cost

The crew had stayed and they were paid
The Doctor, Brute and Feral Maid
They sailed the seas, explored the shore
The Captain and his paramour

Open Skies

The stars above were all alight
As sunset phased into the night
The cows were out, in golden fields
And safe behind protective shields

Behind the clouds, the moon was new
And shimmered with a hazy blue
As up above and all around
The forcefield went from sky to ground

As Henry sat upon his steed
The clouds held warnings he would heed
Leather strong and whiskey dry
Enough to make a grown man cry

The yellow golds to darkened hue
The owls now hooting was his cue
As he rode, he sang and drank
And only had his God to thank

In life this cowboy knew his place
An easy grin, a grizzled face
His herd was calm when sky was clear
He was a man who held no fear

And from his home he was not far
A stone's throw from the nearest bar
But Henry liked the great outdoors
Preferred the dirt to hard wood floors.

A quiet man, a soul of stone
Preferred to spend his time alone
And all was still 'neath gloaming moon
But something cold was coming soon

Off his horse Ol' Henry climbed
The grassland was now cold and rimed

His boots they crunched as tack removed
The horse relaxed, remained unmoved

And as he lay in rolls of fur
The still night air began to stir
Horizons dark were filed with fire
As if the gods released their ire

Burning gold and cobalt blues
Lit the sky in strangest hues
Falling things they hit his shield
He thanked his God it would not yield

A long time ago when the old suns were new
A star exploded and fell like the dew
A torrent of dreams were drawn as a shade
In crimson and gold it started to fade

He had once seen what lay beyond
A few klicks passed the sturgeons' pond
Where grassland twists and turns to sand
Where old gods went and burned the land

This tiny town now lay within
Protected by the thinnest skin
Built before he had been born
A world not known he could not mourn

As witness to these falling stones
He felt it deep within his bones
Something shook, and burned the sky
A growing storm he'd not deny

When morning came, sirens he heard
So the outside world sent word!
He tacked his horse and mounted fast
And rode across green prairies vast

The crowds were huge for this small place
But Henry's horse had set a pace

The groups parted as he passed through
He tipped his hat to those he knew

The townsfolk knew him well indeed
And also recognized his steed
He didn't speak a single word
So all their whispers could be heard

They spoke about his lonesome ways
Out in the fields, they know he stays
He never fights or causes harm
But will show up for an alarm

In the centre of this tiny town
Off of his horse Henry climbed down
The Mayor stood in suit and tie
As if he was about to lie

"The Barrier might face a breach
To you good folks, I now beseech,
In better times the laws were clear
Hold close to those that we hold dear,"

The Mayor spoke with shaky voice
His quiet tone refused a choice
They were to stay from boundary's edge
It was unsafe he did allege

Along open trails far deep in the void
To travel so far they weren't overjoyed
But suns will burn out and fade into black
They'd journeyed so far and could not look back

Henry thought that this was strange
He'd spent much time out on that range
There were some cliffs and rivers deep,
He'd often go there just to sleep

He cleared his throat and raised his hand
The Mayor offered him the stand

"If it's not safe, I can go see,
What kind of danger there might be,"

The murmurs came and chose that course
That Henry would leave on his horse
Search the boundary and keep it clear
Alert if peril ventures near

So off he went with plan in mind
Not knowing, out there, what he'd find
The sun was high but overcast
And Henry did remain steadfast

The paths around the rim he traced
When he had some cows misplaced
Ridges narrow and canyons wide
He knew the best places to hide

Lightning struck and sparked the shield
If rip was caused, it soon was healed
The rain it came like through a sieve
Protection was not all it'd give

Down into valleys Ol' Henry went
Until the light was all but spent
Shallow caves he knew were dry
Were just the place for him to lie

And of the shield that's tinted blue
It did remain within his view
He watched the fires fall once more
Unlike anything seen before

Henry stood while still so tired
To do the job for which he's hired
At the edge with gun in hand
Saw silver ships tear up the land

The siren's squealing pierced the night
While Henry wanted to take flight

Within the flames were hints of green
And shimmered like spilt gasoline

A starburst of time as galaxies passed
A species survived; how long could it last?
A tiny blue speck, so distant a place
A miniscule world so far out in space

He stood so close and touched the shield
Its static skin refused to yield
It rippled underneath his hand
Across the edges where it spanned

Between the trees beyond the edge
Beneath a thorny barren hedge
He saw a face that met his gaze
Somewhere in that bluish haze

The being waved a single hand,
Before it deemed it safe to stand
He wore a suit of silver white
The only soul in Henry's sight

It's skin was pale, and faintly green
The strangest eyes he'd ever seen
Toward the shield Ol' Henry stepped
Upon it though, his sight was kept

With shield between their eyes had met
A moment they would not forget
The stranger touched the forcefield's side
But there were rules he must abide

It recoiled and clutched its chest
It looked like it had needed rest
He could see blood but not in red
"Do you need help?" Ol' Henry said

The creature spoke with trembling tones
Words Henry felt within his bones

He raised his hand and pointed north
To show the stream, and then set forth

Side by side without a word
And Henry still was self-assured
This wounded soul who needed aid
Who should have been here to invade

He kept their pace, and it was brisk
The cowboy knew this was a risk
But Henry saw the stranger's eyes
And in them he had sensed no lies

The stream was close, just one more ridge
It wasn't big, there was no bridge
They reached the crest and looked below
The water black and flowing slow

The blue of this world was far beyond dreams
A gem in the darkness and oh, how it gleams
A treasure, a gift, the most precious of stones
All that remained would be ashes and bones

The shield just touched the surface here
Beneath the stream if they'd adhere
To what they had been told to do
The soul would find the passage through

Henry showed it where to swim
The look he got was read as grim
In the stream Ol' Henry stepped
And on that side, the creature leapt

In seconds Henry grasped its arm
The plan had worked just like a charm
Henry pulled them to the sand
The two then sat down on the land

Henry reached and touched its wound
It pulled away and clicked and crooned

It stood up swift but winced in pain
And Henry reached out once again

The stranger stared back quite confused
"You seemed to be a little bruised"
Henrys voice was soft and calm
He lifted up an open palm

"This fire fell down from the sky,
Explain it all and don't be shy."
In Henry's mind, the creature spoke
"I'm thankful to all helpful folk"

Its words were slow and had a lilt
And it explained how blood was spilt
Of wars and stars, a search for gold
Of ancient glories yet untold

The two suns set on their old world
Around which several moons once whirled
So they had left when times were dire
Seen their last home consumed by fire

It told him of their plans for earth
The voice remained devoid of mirth
Escapes it made were on its own
And into danger he'd been thrown

His leaders knew of his betrayal
And they would kill him without fail
So, to the human race he went
To help had been his one intent

With thousands of eyes to see and behold
They drew information into the fold
An epoch of war, of blood and disease
Of worshiping gods they'd never appease

Ol Henry sat, and thought quite hard
He knew he had to be on guard

But kindly eyes and gentle tone
This cowboy now felt less alone

The vastness of this prairie farm
Had never been a cause for alarm
Even when the shield went up
Before he even was a pup

For now the light was growing dim
The being cold from his small swim
So with the steed they both went back
Followed Henry's well trekked track

The homestead cold, from lack of use
The generator had no juice
The stranger made adjustments few
The house was then lit up like new

But as they talked and Henry yawned
A thought that crept finally dawned
"Oh, you don't sleep," poor Henry said,
"Yet I could rest just like the dead."

Henry stood and stretched himself
"There's food and drink upon that shelf,"
"Just don't leave, there's much to say
I would prefer it if you'd stay,"

The being bowed, and Henry slept
To watch the house, its promise kept
And soon the sun began to rise
The being never closed i eyes

The sky was blue and open wide
Henry's fear would soon subside
But still the town would need to learn
Beyond the shield their world would burn

He packed his horse, the saddle tacked
And made a list of what he lacked

The Knight Witch

The being watched with those strange eyes
Ol' Henry thought they seemed so wise

"So you should stay, the town will see
There has not been harm done to me
But I am sure they will react,
This means I must go showing tact,"

A promise was made, this planet was claimed
A lush fertile world that still wasn't named
A single bright star would keep them all warm
And this tiny world midst the eye of the storm

His mighty steed was moving slow
Ignored the sun still sitting low
Ol' Henry focused on the road
And moved just like the river flowed

As he approached, the town was still
He had his list he must fulfil
And not too far there was a store
They called it "Ye olde Hungry Boar"

It wasn't closed, he went inside
He walked the shelves to then decide
The owner watched him with a glare
It wasn't like he'd not been there

With furrowed brow he asked the clerk
"Just having a hard day at work?"
His wrinkled face would only nod
Though concerned he dared not prod

Beside the door the sheriff stood,
A man he'd known since childhood
His black hat now was tilted down
Upon his face the deepest frown

Henry smiled and tipped his hat
He knew they were about to chat

The Sheriff's smile was cold at best
His badge was glinting on his chest

"I saw that you had made it back,"
To see the truth he had a knack
Ol' Henry saw he shouldn't lie
Omit some truths he'd have to try

"I surely did, I found the trails"
And Henry skipped a few details
"No breach was found, of that I'm sure,
The shield it still remains secure."

The Sheriff spat and kicked the sand
"This best be truth by God's own hand,"
Henry shrugged, "Hope to die,
"Stick a needle in my eye,"

The childish phrase it woke a grin
Ol' Henry would confess that sin
The Sheriff then had turned his cheek
As he had no more words to speak

The world had been burned by humans alone
Some places yet green, the rest dry as bone
Covetous eyes had wanted much more
They would lay claim even if it meant war

Ol' Henry bought all his supplies
He noticed costs were on the rise
Fear made people quick to buy
Prices rose for short supply

Henry packed his horse to go
The locals wandered to and froe
And worried eyes would fall on him
Their outlooks were now cold and grim

A second passed and he could see
A gun in his periphery

Upon a roof not far away
Ol' Henry he knew not to stay

The sheriff thought to have him watched
It was a plan that now was botched
He checked his hip and found his gun
But wouldn't shoot, he'd have to run

Down the road a silhouette
And it was shaped like a regret
Hands outstretched and quick to draw
At least that's what Ol' Henry saw

He mounted up and gave a nod
The horse took off without a prod
The Sheriff came in from the west
Ol' Henry saw this was a test

If he had dared to leave at pace
They would shoot and then give chase
A storm was brewing inside the shield
It wasn't time for him to yield

Ol' Henry left and hit the trail
He saw the sheriff on his tail
Before his path they could impede
Henry's horse had gathered speed

Their eyes on him their focus fixed
In trouble he had now been mixed
But he went forth, his head held high
It was not him now doomed to die

A gunshot rose and pierced the air
Ol' Henry he had stopped to stare
A warning shot he was quite sure
But their intentions were not pure

Rivals were made during trials by fire
Then some became mercenaries for hire

For whatever price seemed to offer them more
Resulted in so much bloodshed and gore

"Sheriff, my friend, I know your name
I don't know if this is a game,"
Both Henry's hands were raised up high
But felt his gun against his thigh

He counted three more in his sight
And they were ready for a fight
But Henry kept his movements clear
They would not shoot him out of fear

They mostly had the upper hand
For this is how they had it planned
And still he walked into their trap
But not much more he'd take their crap

The Sheriff spat and then he grinned
Then Ol' Henry's patience thinned
"Between your teeth a traitor's tongue"
The Sheriff thought his words had stung

Ol' Henry looked from man to man
His face it had remained deadpan
If just one soul had taken aim
This Cowboy would just have his name

So Henry watched for other signs
A signal in the shield confines
Above their heads far past the shield
The ships appeared above the field

The Sherriff followed Henry's gaze
"What kind of hell you tryin' to raise?"
Ol' Henry had to drop his hands
This Sheriff had sold out these lands

Henry grabbed the reins and yelled
The tension in the air had swelled

The Sheriff's guns lit up the sky
Their simple plan had gone awry

Henry's horse it fled the scene
To pastures that were far more green
And not once did he pull his gun
They aimed to kill and not to stun

The Sheriff called to chase him down
To bring his body back to the town
But Henry knew the lands so well
He knew the routes to give them hell

A promise was made by those on the ground
When it was open, they'd not make a sound
The Sheriff knew that blood would be spilled
But would look away if his family weren't killed

Henry rode on from hillock to tree
When they missed, he dodged the debris
By single hairs at every turn
The hardest target they would learn

The first one fell, their horse stopped hard
And he had been caught off his guard
Over ears with no reigns to hold
Then off a ledge the henchman rolled

Henry watched them pass him by
Left their comrade there to die
No guilt, concern or spoken word
Perhaps his cry they had not heard

Their focus was on Henry still
Just one outlaw they'd try to kill
But he was quick, despite his age
The sheriff descended into rage

Random shots from every side
And all he had to do was ride

While up above more ships appeared
And in his mind their lights were seared

Ol' Henry knew to grab his gun
And take them all out one by one
Just two more heads to watch go down
He'd stop it all and save the town

Now Henry he was running hot
The next one down had caught the shot
From chest to neck he felt the blow
The bloody wounds began to flow

Howls rang from the Sheriff's mouth
His campaign was now headed south
As Henry rode and kicked up dirt
He knew he had to make him hurt

Out west the smoke was rising high
A column straight into the sky
Something burned not far away
Then sparks flew out in coloured spray

Ol' Henry knew where that path led
The station where the shield was fed
Protection for their tiny town
The sheriff planned to bring it down

Timeless desires and needs to survive
Keeps even the weakest human alive
But what of a race who fights to the end
Who carries no man, not even a friend

The Sheriff with his star so bright
Hadn't given up the fight
Henry raced and urged his steed
Through a patch of dried-up weed

Shield controls were near the pond
Passed a hedge, and just beyond

He felt a shot graze past his arm
One inch left would do him harm

The laser blast had burned his shirt
But he for now had not been hurt
He fired back without much care
The Sheriff wasn't even there

So Henry looked out to his right
And now he had him in his sight
His hat was gone and poured with sweat
Ol' Henry hadn't beat him yet

Up above the shield had faded
The generator had been raided
He had to go and fix what's broke
The sheriff had a flame to stoke

So neck and neck they raced their steeds
Hoping that the other bleeds
Ol' Henry shot at his old friend
To bring this to a bitter end

Ahead Ol' Henry saw the site
Two men had set it all alight
And though it shook him to his core
With two shots they'd breathe no more

The Sheriff turned with eyes of fire
This would come down to the wire
But Henry's face was cold as steel
As if he knew not how to feel

Far above the ships closed in
It seemed as though he could not win
But cowboys know the day's not done
Until the sinking of the sun

The generator room was locked
The Sheriff grinned with gun half-cocked

Henry turned and fired fast
His dear old friend would breathe his last

From far distant stars these creatures had flown
Into the depth of the darkness unknown
This smallish blue world with touches of green
Would give them a fight like they'd never seen

He put the flames out where he could
The building had been mostly wood
The door was breached the lights were out
Of fixing this there was some doubt

A voice cried out but not with words
'Twas almost like the sounds of birds
Ol' Henry looked and then he smiled
This being now had him beguiled

It touched the screens and dials too
Within those eyes it seemed it knew
Above they heard the first attack
Reverberating thunder crack

The two locked eyes, the work begun
All Henry had was just his gun
He watched the door and then the sky
So many folk were gonna die

He watched the shield and as it failed
Into their space a craft had sailed
It shone so bright with steel and chrome
And then he saw it gone, the dome

Beyond the sky he saw the stars
Like fireflies in mason jars
Where twilight meets the dawn's new glow
He thought he was about to go

Then he felt a searing pain
From his shoulder to his brain

He looked and saw the Sheriff's grin
That look from one about to win

Ol' Henry smiled with twisted lip
And pulled his iron from his hip
"Just one more shot and you could lose"
His blood was dripping on his shoes

"Ol' Henry, you could never know
The world beyond your fire's glow."
The Sherriff spat into the soil
This cowboy's blood was on the boil

With one clear shot the game was won
But this bad day was far from done
The badge he wore Ol' Henry took
And gave it just a quiet look

Emergency calls rang out through the craft
Now less of a ship and more of a raft
As fire engulfed and tore them asunder
The last thing they heard was a torrent of thunder

All was still for a second to mourn
Before all the craft from the sky were torn
A familiar hum had come from inside
Henry turned and then beamed with pride

Those starry eyes filled with relief
But somewhere it was mixed with grief
Far up above cold metal was rending
It was the town they were defending

Ships broke in two, the shield returned
So many of them crashed and burned
Ol' Henry watched the open skies
So bright he had to close his eyes

The being reached with open hand
Ol' Henry felt he couldn't stand

So down the wall he slowly slid
Kind of proud of what he did

The wound was fresh and bleeding fast
He wasn't sure that he would last
But time and wounds are intertwined
And to his fate he was resigned

A gentle hand upon his head
Removed the bloody stains of red
His breathing eased and now so deep
No longer felt like he should sleep

It helped him stand on his own feet
What it had done had worked a treat
The world still burned outside this room
With creatures still to meet their doom

The air was filled with smoke so thick
It made them both start feeling sick
So on his horse, Henry did ride
The being there right by his side

And to the town with news to share
For anyone who was still there
The road was smooth but metal flecked
Chunks of steel would soon be checked

No souls it seemed survived the crash
But thoughts like that could be too rash
And as the two arrived in town
All Henry did was stare and frown

Of silver and steel and burning with red
Many were counted and numbered as dead
Though all had seemed lost, they would not yield
They were protected by more than a shield

No news to give, they already knew
Now the sky shone, and shimmered blue

The Knight Witch

They counted dead, and who was maimed
Even a soul they couldn't have named

Now they had drinks, sorrows to drown
They'd be fine once more in this town
And then rebuild this place once more
And mending things the metal tore

Supplies were lost during the chase
And while fighting outer space
He asked for more, they understood
Gave him more than what they should

With goods in hand he packed his horse
And let the being join in of course
By all accounts, he owed a debt
And one that he could not regret

So, on the trail, it shared no words
While Henry talked of tending herds
Spoke of plants that roll with the wind
And he explained how beans were tinned

The sunset came in golds and green
And still it had a bluish sheen
The home was still and yet unmarred
Only the town had ended scarred

Those starry eyes had seen so much
And yet it wasn't out of touch
Ol' Henry shared his food and house
The being quiet as a mouse

It served him well as days went by
Both their eyes stayed on the sky
Ol' Henry knew it understood
And he was sure that things were good

The air was warm, the whiskey dry
Horizons showed the clear blue sky

As Henry lay to fall asleep
A watch he knew his friend would keep

As Henry stared and counted stars
Like fireflies in mason jars
As his sleep he tried to stave
His friend inferred *a second wave.*

About the Author

Ten years ago, Suzanne Jayne Bradley showed up at a friend's thirtieth birthday party dressed as a poet. Fortunately, the theme of the party was "What you wanted to be when you grew up" and no one who knows her was surprised by Suzanne's choice, because her love of writing and poetry is long-standing.

She has been crafting poems since primary school and at sixteen even won third place in a high school writing competition (for a little tiny poem of no consequence, but she's still proud of it!).

Over the years, Suzanne has worked various jobs, from cafés to call centres and even on film shoots. Currently, she lives in Auckland, New Zealand, working in an office for a manufacturing company while continuing to nurture her love of writing.

With her second book now published, she is committed to her new dream of writing poetry for a living. Finger's crossed!

Works by S Jayne Bradley

Clocks Locks Corpses!: And Other Epic Horror Poems
(Sir Julius Vogel Award Finalist – 2025)

The Knight Witch: and Other Epic Poems